THE
WABELE

by

CHRISTOPHER MALINGER

ISBN – 13: 978-0990701828
ISBN – 10: 0990701824

DEDICATION

This book is dedicated to my grandparents,
Vincent and Helen, who gave me the most
memorable summers on Kangaroo Lake in
Door County, Wisconsin.

ACKNOWLEDGMENTS

Eileen Malinger
Jonathan Malinger
Sean Malinger
Tommy and Trevor Prondzinski
Door County Library
Florida Writers Association

Jacket design by Eileen Malinger

Cover photograph: tobkatrina/Shutterstock.com

INTRODUCTION

Having spent many summers in Door County, at my grandparent's cottage on Kangaroo Lake, I look back on those years with fond memories. The events, people, and some of the geographical locations are mere creations of my imagination and only used to enhance my story. Any similarities to persons living, or dead, are purely coincidental. My affection for Door County, and its people, will always have a special place in my heart.

THE WABELE

Think in the morning that perhaps you won't

survive until evening, and in the evening that

perhaps you won't survive until morning.

—Quote from the Paris Catacombs

"Give it to me," Tommy Roberts yelled to Trevor. Instead, Trevor taunted his brother by gyrating around him, always keeping a safe distance from his grasp.

Trevor's lankly frame moved agilely on the attic's dust-laden floorboards. As he jumped, an occasional squeak from the planks cried out, adding to the commotion. On his head he wore a wood contrivance that resembled a helmet, but it wasn't a helmet. It looked like the unworldly merger of crocodiles, and boars with a devilish guidance in its assembly. The crocodiles sprung from both sides of the headpiece intertwined with the tusks of boars; the whole piece topped with a few more horns. Its base colors of red and black were interspersed with contrasting white and red horizontal and vertical dots. The demonic diadem devoured much of Trevor's head, barely allowing him to see Tommy's covetous hands.

"It's my turn!" Tommy begged.

Trevor was beginning to tire of the weight on his head, so he stopped and removed the piece, offering it to his envious brother. "Here, take it," he said, holding it out to him.

"Wait, I want to do something else with it," Tommy said, temporarily declining the offer. Taking the white cotton sheet that draped over the chest, where they found the headpiece, he placed it over his entire body and imagined himself as a ghost. "Now put it on my head," he said to his brother, his voice muffled under the sheet.

Trevor obeyed. After it was in place, Tommy began to move about the attic, emitting muted ghost sounds. "OOOOH ooooh ahhhh ahhhh," he moaned, attempting to frighten his brother. Tommy lacked the clarity of vision within the sheet, so his sightless movements were guarded.

The deception became more comedic than scary because of Tommy's blindness. After nearly tripping on the sheet, he called for help. "Trevor! Get this thing off of me."

As Trevor began to approach his brother a chill swept through the cavernous loft. It was an unusual draft of air, like the one that washes over you when opening the freezer door on a hot summer day, but more intense. It lingered only for a moment before being swept away by a warm Wisconsin gust that channeled its way up from the open attic door below.

"Did you feel that?" Trevor asked, helping to remove the headpiece.

"Yeah, it felt kinda creepy," Tommy said, peeking from under the sheet. "Let's put this back in the trunk," he said, while making his way toward the open chest.

"Don't put it in there like that, it went this way," Trevor instructed his brother. "It was resting on its side like this, with the open end facing the lock."

Twins, but not identical in looks or temperament, both enjoyed exploring the contents of the boxes and things accumulated in the attic. Most, not all belonged to their uncle Jonathan. He was an archeologist, a word that was alien in understanding to the boys. He was the closest thing to a father they had. Their father died a couple of years after they were born. Their mother Ruth, never remarried, saying to them, "Why would I, having the two most handsome, and nicest young men living with me now?"

Although the loss of Raymond Roberts was almost eight years ago, Ruth never truly recovered, and was unable to move on. Tall, like her brother, she presented a striking image with her blonde poodle cut hairstyle and Audrey Hepburn like features. Her attractive features became a magnet for would be suitors, but her unresponsiveness to any romantic involvement discouraged any pursuit to flourish.

Her brother, Jonathan would be a regular guest in their house and the attic became a repository for his treasures. The regularity of his visits, her job as the head librarian, and taking care of two boys was enough activity in her life. "Maybe someday, I will, but not now," she would tell her brother, when the subject came up.

Once everything was in order, they put the sheet back over the wooden box. Its similarity to a pirate's treasure chest was reason enough for it to be a magnet for their curiosity. They gave the place the onceover, and made sure the attic looked the same way as they found it. The boys scampered down the stairway. Running outside to play catch, they were unaware of the misfortune that had descended with them.

***

A slight wind stroked the sand dunes of Door County. The peninsula resembled a disjointed skeletal thumb, jutting out into the cold waters of Lake Michigan. Today's weather was the exception, for this point of land knew more turbulent conditions than fair. Even its name meant trouble. The early French explorers called the corridor of water between the northern tip of the peninsula and the Potawatomi Islands, *Porte des Morts Passage*, which in English means "Way to the Door of the Dead." Now it was hosting the play of Angelica, and her dog Chester.

Angelica's blonde hair fluttered in the early morning breeze as she ran along the dry dunes, higher than the tidal wash of its lapping waters. Chester, her gray schnauzer, fast at her heels, scattered sand in his wake. Her laughter blended with his barking and the rhythmic pulse of the surf.

Suddenly Chester froze. His focus was the tree line of pines, set far removed from the shoreline. Angelica, realizing that he was no longer by her side, glanced back. His rigid body was poised at something beyond the string of trees.

"Chester! Come here," she called out, but he ignored her command. "Chester!" she yelled again. Her call went unheeded. Suddenly his body came alive, bolted away from the beach and into the forest. Her repeated calls remained disregarded; the dense foliage of the woods soon swallowed the sound of his barks.

Rather than follow him, she headed toward the lighthouse, the height of which would allow her a better view. Her father was the lighthouse keeper, so her presence on the grounds was not unusual, but entry into the steel tower was—and against her father's orders.

The heavy metal door fought her effort to enter, but her determination to find Chester paid off in the end. Once inside, she sprinted up the circular staircase, her footfalls echoing her progress. Three windows, strategically positioned within the structure, provided the only light along her path. The air inside was musty. After reaching the top she looked through the glass windows that stood defending the inner light from the weather's assaults. Her own reflection prevented her from a clear view of the coastline. Slowly the Fresnel lens followed its circular path, sending out a beam of light to all mariners within range.

Trying to seek a better view, she opened the door to the outside catwalk. The cool stale damp air of the interior rushed past her as she moved outside. Her attention was drawn to the forested land beyond the sand.

"Chester!" her tiny voice swallowed by the sound of the breakers. While scanning the woodlands for any movement she persisted in calling his name. Straining every bit of fiber in her cries she finally stood on the railing's middle rung. Firmly holding the top handrail for support, she leaned forward, pressing her midsection against it.

In the distance, within the shadow of the tree line, a lone figure of a man, no not a man, but that of a clown, stood holding Chester. The sight of a clown was not something she could process, let alone have foreseen. Like a crimson bolt of lightning across a blue sky, it shocked her. A combination of surprise, shoes dampened during her morning run, coupled with the climb on dank lighthouse stairs, caused her to lose traction. Her feet slipped under the protective restraint of the top railing.

Tiny hands, curled around the cold, dew-laden rail, were no help in preventing her tumble. Escaping the safety of the sweeping enclosure, she soon found flight. Her wet hands yanked free from their precarious embrace of the steel. Airborne, her head struck the previous footing. Angelica's head hit with such force, that it rendered her unconscious, sparing her the awareness of the horrific plunge to earth.

***

"Oh my God!" Tommy and Trevor's mother Ruth exclaimed, stopping for a moment, as she prepared scrambled eggs for breakfast.

"What's wrong Mom?" Trevor asked on his way to the kitchen table, noticing a glassy distressed look in his mother's eyes. Tommy, trailing his brother, also observed her sorrow, but remained mute.

"The radio broadcaster just announced that Angelica Barnes died this morning." Fighting to contain her grief, she hesitantly continued, "She fell from the lighthouse at the point. Oh, what a tragedy for the family. That was their only child," she stopped, blotted her eyes with her apron and cleared the lump from her throat.

"They will need emotional help during this time. Angelica's funeral will probably be this Friday. We will all go to show our support," she said, examining the boys for any reaction. They knew Angelica from school, although a grade behind them. "Mrs. Barnes was a regular at the library," she said, but her statement was more reflective on how life will change for the Barnes' family, remembering her own loss eight years earlier.

***

A child's funeral can be beyond the scope of understanding God's will. Chief Barnes wore his Coast Guard dress-blue uniform, and Mrs. Barnes covered herself in a black mourning dress; both were grief-stricken with self-blame. All of the Coast Guard detachment from the lighthouse and nearby station attended, with the exception of the personnel manning the watch. Most of the town's inhabitants were present. The loss of one among the few, particularly a child, resulted in communal bereavement. In addition, Father's Day was only two days away and would have a sorrow of its own.

After the funeral Mass, Tommy and Trevor Roberts faded into the perimeter of the church hall following the luncheon. Finding little occasion for conversation with the adults, they talked between themselves. A few of their fellow classmates were also there, but stayed close to their own parents. Ruth, dressed in a navy blue sundress with small white polka dots, floated among the mourners, offering emotional comfort to the family and friends.

"That's the first time I ever saw a dead kid," Trevor remarked to his brother.

"It felt scary to me," Tommy replied. "I'll probably have bad dreams now. What about you?"

"I really don't know, Tom. I think we should keep the desk light on tonight." Trevor nodded and studied the floor in silence.

Later, back at home, neither one felt eager to play, or do anything that resembled recreation. Tommy read a book on spiders, or more correctly, looked at the pictures. Occasionally he glanced out the open window to the right of his bed.

Trevor, the artist of the family, grabbed a sketchpad, and while resting in bed, doodled. Positioned between both beds stood a small desk, on which rested a table lamp. It cast a cone of light onto its surface, and partially spilling over to the linoleum covered floor. On Trevor's left, another partially opened window allowed a slight breeze to drift through the bedroom

"Tommy," Trevor stopped his sketching and called out to his brother. "Do you think Angelica felt any pain?"

Tommy placed the book, open side down on his lap, "Don't really know, but if she did, I bet it was quick."

That answer satisfied Trevor and he resumed drawing.

***

The tranquility of the late spring night compelled the boys to sleep with both screened windows partially open, encouraging the wind, no matter how slight, to travel through their room. The night air was warm for an early June evening, so Tommy and Trevor slept only in their pajama bottoms.

Midway through the night, the waning moon's crescent shown itself high in the night sky, adding little light to the landscape below. A slight draught of air, midway through the night, followed an angular path crosswise between the windows, which caused Tommy to reach for the thin sheet at the foot of his bed. Half asleep, he glanced toward the window alongside Trevor's bed.

Framed in the opening, skirted by wispy drapes, stood Angelica, pale and motionless, appearing unhappy. She looked beyond the limits of the room, past Tommy. Although silent, her lips appeared to move, as if she was talking to someone, maybe to him, he wasn't sure.

"Trevor! Trevor! Get up!" he yelled, frightened by the vision standing beyond the windowsill.

Trevor began to stir, with eyes half open looked in Tommy's direction. "What wrong?" He opened his eyes completely, and stared directly at his brother, while remaining reclined.

"Look!" he pointed. "It's Angelica! She's outside your window."

Looking at his window, seeing nothing, he regarded his brother skeptically. He only saw Tommy cowered at the foot of his bed, staring at the open window.

"Go back to sleep Tommy, it was only a bad dream."

Tommy looked at Trevor and back at the window; the apparition was gone. Watching the opening, with the expectation of Angelica's reappearance, he eventually tired and returned to an uneasy sleep.

***

Trevor was the first one to the breakfast table. "Tommy had a bad dream last night, Mom. He said that he saw Angelica outside his window."

"I'm sure it was only a nightmare. Going to a funeral is never a pleasant thing and he only imagined seeing her," Mrs. Roberts replied, trying to reduce the anxiety in the boys' first exposure to death of someone they knew.

Tommy entered the kitchen without saying a word. It was obvious that he had something on his mind because his silence was out of character. His stillness was a concern for Ruth.

"Trevor told me that you saw Angelica through the window last night," she said, trying to coax a conversation with him.

"Don't know. Maybe it was a bad dream. She looked real to me, and it scared me. I don't want to talk about it. Okay?" His tone was unyielding, prompting silence from his mother and brother. They ate quietly, except for the occasional request of breakfast items to be passed.

After breakfast, Ruth hurried off to work at the library. It was Trevor's turn to clean up after the meal, so Tommy, in his desire for solitude, hopped on his bike and headed toward the beach.

It was a good feeling to fight the wind that came off the lake. Rapidly pumping the pedals, his lungs struggled to gulp air as it raced past. He didn't want to think of anything except speed.

Hitting the crest of the dunes, he began to lose momentum. He fought the pressure of the sand's resistance to topple him. Eventually he gave in to the heaviness of his bike tires in the clinging sand and stopped. His dismount was awkward, nearly falling as the bike slowed. He left it where it stopped.

Sitting on top of the ridge, he was almost obscured by the beachgrass, which surrounded him. His perch on an isthmus of bare sand, offered limited access to the view below of the surf. The grass, encouraged by the lake's wind, swirled around him.

Alone with his thoughts, his attention was drawn to a young woman strolling the beach. Her presence was not unusual, because many tourists walked along the shoals, and sands of the lake. What was unusual was the clothing. She wore clothes similar to those worn by his great-grandmother whose picture hung on his living room wall. The woman, sporting a large-brim hat, was outfitted in a flowing amber dress, with matching top, and accented with a white lace border. The full-length dress obscured her shoes and gave the impression of a person gliding over the sand. She left no tracks in the sand.

He stood up in an effort to get a better look. His sudden emergence from the dune went unnoticed by her. She continued to walk along the beach, and appeared to be crying and never looked in his direction. Curious about the woman, Tommy gathered his bike and began to follow, but at a distance.

He was able to push his bike more freely when he reached the moist sand, which made it easier for him to shadow her. Ahead, and approaching, Tommy saw another individual. Once close enough, he saw it was a man, dressed in a denim work uniform of some type, dripping wet with a crimson colored forehead, moving wearily forward.

Tommy stopped, looked at the man, but didn't receive any acknowledgement. The stranger continued to walk on a fixed route, never altering his forward gaze. His discolored brow now revealed more detail; his head was partially caved in. Tommy, frightened, looked toward the woman again and observed only the empty beach, and the lighthouse on the point; she simply vanished. Looking backward in the direction of the retreating man, Tommy saw only the lapping waves upon a deserted shoreline.

Confused, Tommy looked in the direction of the lighthouse. High above the shoreline, a lone figure of a little girl leaned on the railing that surrounded the light. She appeared to be looking for something, not out toward the lake, but inland, toward the forest. Suddenly she too disappeared.

Overcome with panic he jumped on his bike; riding back through the sand like it wasn't there. He did not stop until he was within sight of his white picket fence. After yanking open the gate, he threw the bike alongside of the path leading to the house. Breathless, he charged toward the entrance and the safety within, letting the screen door slam shut behind.

"Trevor! Trevor! Where are you?" yelled Tommy.

"Whaddya want?" asked his brother, emerging from their bedroom.

"I think I see ghosts!"

"You mean like Casper?" Trevor asked mockingly.

"No, dead people from long ago and I saw Angelica again. She was standing on top of the lighthouse at the point." He was close to hysterics and aware his claims would sound unbelievable. "Honestly, I see 'em,", Tommy pleaded, trying to convince his brother of his seriousness.

Tommy went into the kitchen and his brother followed. He opened the refrigerator and retrieved a bottle of Coke. Using a bottle opener he popped the lid, poured some into a glass, and offered the half-empty bottle to Trevor. Trevor took a swallow, and studied his brother, uncertain of his mental state.

"Okay, tell me what you saw."

Tommy told his story, with Trevor fascinated by the idea of seeing the dead. After he finished, Trevor said, "Cool, we can hang around the cemetery, and you can tell me what you see?"

"I ain't going anywhere near that creepy place," Tommy fired back.

"You gonna tell Mom?"

"Dunno, maybe. What do you think I should do?"

"Maybe you should, tonight, after supper," was the only advice Trevor could give.

***

Preparing dinner was usually a family affair, and because their mother worked late, sometimes the twins had to peel potatoes, shuck corn, or clean vegetables. Tonight's meal was a treat for everyone since their mother was stopping at Bailey's for a takeout of fish and chips.

"You boys are unusually quiet tonight. What have you been up to? I hope you're not going to tell me you broke something?" Her questions caused the boys to glance at one another, hoping the other would start the conversation.

"Err...I think...I —" Tommy started, but was cut off by Trevor.

"Tommy can see ghosts, Mom!"

Their mother's attention quickly became fixed on Tommy, who was now silent. "What does that mean; you 'can see ghosts?'"

Realizing Trevor's claim required some type of answer, Tommy began to tell his story while his meal rapidly cooled. Finished, he resumed eating, but with less enthusiasm, waiting for his mom's reaction.

"Well, that is quite a story," she began, carefully selecting her words, offering some parental insight. "Sometimes people think they see things that are not there. You had a bad dream last night, and maybe that has something to do with what you think you saw. Imagination is a powerful thing; it can control you, making you believe something is real."

Changing the subject, she said, "Let's clean up the kitchen together and watch the Perry Mason show tonight. I'll even make some popcorn."

When dinner cleanup was done, and before the popcorn was made, the twins' mother had an idea. "Maybe we all should go to the circus tomorrow in Stevens Point?" she said, eyeing the boys for a reaction. They both perked up at the idea. She added, "Maybe we all need a change of scenery."

***

"Hey, Rube!" The circus worker bellowed, running after the kid who stole his cash box. "Stop! You son of a bitch."

"Rube?" Jacob Rubenstein thought, as he hurled himself into the circus crowd, hoping to get lost in their numbers, *"How does he know my name?"* The cash box rattled under his arm as his worn shoes kicked up a cloud of dirt. The noise and dust made him an easy target for his pursuers to follow.

"Hey, Rube!" A fat, unkempt-looking circus worker, with two days growth of beard, called out again as he labored a breath in pursuit. Soon other workers converged on his cries of *hey Rube*, which was the universal call for assistance between circus and carnival people. Jacob's eyes darted about in search of an exit.

Making a sharp turn to his right he found a dead end of tents and trailers; there was no place to hide. He was boxed in. Suddenly a figure emerged from the shadows; it was a clown.

Silently, but with great expression, the clown jumped back and forth in his oversized shoes waving his hands wildly in the air, prompting Jacob to follow.

With an angry crowd of circus workers on his heels, the seemingly nonthreatening buffoon appeared to be his only alternative. As Jacob approached, the clown pulled back a flap of the tent and enticed the fleeing boy to enter.

The flap closed behind Jacob, and the black interior of the tent swooped around him, leaving him in nothingness. His straining eyes tried to adjust to the darkness, but not so much as a sliver of light broke through the blackness. He heard the muffled sounds of agitated people, but the words were without form. He held out his arm in an attempt to find something solid by which he could get his bearings. The other arm clutched the moneybox. Carefully inching his way forward, his shoes scraped across the uneven ground, unsure of the ground's stability.

Abruptly a streak of light shot into the dark interior and grew, soon overwhelming the inside of the tent. With it, a crush of circus workers descended upon Jacob.

"Steal from us you little bastard!" one of the men shouted.

The boy found the moneybox ripped from his grip then felt the pummels of the mob. Cut and bruised, he was ejected from the tent with a warning, "Don't come back here again if you know what's good for ya."

The clown, standing beyond the melee, smiled approvingly of the justice served. Taking an oversized handkerchief from one of his cavernous pockets, he pretended to mime sadness; blotting make-believe tears from his large, villainous eyes. As Jacob was thrown out, the clown waved the kerchief in the air, mocking the boy's expulsion. Jacob glared back at him.

"It looks like you've earned your keep already, Mister Devlin," said the

Tent Master approvingly. "Welcome to our family."

Mister Devlin smiled, with hands clasped over his heart, over-dramatizing his acknowledgement of the appreciation. Everyone laughed, and then returned to the business of the circus. Yes, he had indeed found a home.

***

The family's ride along the east coast of Door County was uneventful. The highway, set far inland, only offered a couple of glimpses of Lake Michigan. That suited Ruth Roberts just fine; the purpose of the trip was to get young minds off the lake, lighthouses, and ghosts.

Smells from hay, canvas, sisal rope, and cotton candy wafted among the throng of circus goers. Amid the clamor, occasionally a bell chimed, indicating that someone had attained a feat of skill. Barkers yelled, exhorting the gullible to leave the passing throng and spend money at their locations. Laughter, squeals of delight, all blended with the sounds of animals, creating a cacophony of diversion. If distraction was the objective of this trip, it was proving to be a success.

The boys feasted on hot dogs, roasted corn-on-the-cob, popcorn, and all varieties of candies. Their mother also enjoyed the fare, but at a slower pace and in more sensible moderation. After eating, their tummies were turned and twirled in instruments of torture, sadistically labeled fun rides. Their mother sat at a distance, taking in the joy the boys experienced.

The last thing on the list of things to do was the Big Top show. Ruth Roberts followed her fatigued boys into the spacious tent. Being among the first people to enter, they found ringside seats and eagerly awaited the show to begin. She wondered about the twins' stomach capacity, surprised by their clamorous request for peanuts from a passing vendor.

After the lights dimmed in the viewing stands a single spotlight beam fell onto the center ring. "Ladies and gentlemen, children of all ages, welcome to the *Circus Fantastic!*" the ringmaster proclaimed. His pronouncement resulted in thunderous applause and screams of excitement.

What followed were entertainment offerings ranging from animal acts to high-wire performances. Comic relief was in the form of a group of clowns pouring out of an undersized fire truck to extinguish a fire. Rather than water, their buckets contained confetti, which was liberally doused on each other, and some members of the audience.

The walk-around gags of the make-believe fire brigade left center ring to the approving roars of the crowd. Once they were clear of the hippodrome's track, beyond the ring, darkness descended. The only light came from the exit signs. A mysterious glow began to intensify at the hub of the showground, illuminating Mister Devlin, the newest member of the traveling circus.

Standing under the radiance of the Big Top, Mister Devlin paused in apparent contemplation. His bulbous red nose, bright as a rising sun, aimed high into the blackness of the tent's dark recesses. He slowly pivoted his head from side to side, drawing in the crowd, his indigo blue hair rippling between shadow and light as he turned. In this stillness of anticipation, his melancholic eyes probed the audience, his stare never broken.

Bending forward at the waist, arms outstretched in humble repose, he bowed fleetingly, then just as quickly, resumed an upright posture, his red multi-layered collar flaying about by his abrupt change in posture. Saying nothing, he walked outside the halo of light. Returning after a brief moment, he pulled a large chest into the glow with over expressive mime gestures. He mesmerized the assembly within the tent into silence, everyone waiting in anxious anticipation of what he will do next.

"Trevor," Tommy whispered.

"Yeah, whaddya want?"

Tommy's face got within inches of Trevor's, and cupping his hand over his mouth to guard his words, saying, "That clown is evil. I can see it."

Trevor turned to his brother in surprise. "You afraid of clowns now, too? Leave me alone, I want to watch the show."

Meanwhile, Mister Devlin opened the trunk with silent fanfare revealing to the crowd that the box was empty. To Ruth Roberts' surprise, and her twins, he began to approach them with an extended hand, inviting participation in his act. With a wave of his hand he gestured to Tommy to step forward, but Tommy avoided looking directly at him. Sensing his reluctance, the clown changed his attention toward Trevor, who was only too happy to follow.

"Don't go, Trevor. He's evil," Tommy implored, while trying to hold back his brother. The crowd laughed at Tommy's apparent fear.

"Don't be silly Tommy. It's only an act," their mother softly rebuked his objection and gently pried loose Tommy's grip on his brother's arm.

Disregarding the cautions of his brother, Trevor eagerly accepted the invitation of Mister Devlin, and became bathed, ring center, in the glow. The crowd began to clap in admiration, but the clown waved down the applause, silencing the gathering.

Coaxed into the chest, Trevor stood showered in light, and the center of attention, relishing every moment. Mister Devlin gently patted the top of Trevor's head, indicating he wanted him to crouch down as he began to close the trunk lid.

After the top was secure, the clown moved around the box several times with numerous hand-gesturing embellishments. After circling, the light focused its beam on the chest, went dark for a second, then flooded the container, and Mister Devlin.

The clown, after intentionally pausing to heighten the suspense, flung open the lid, whereupon all four sides outwardly collapsed open. The box was empty. Trevor appeared to have vanished. Mister Devlin looked shocked; pulling out his handkerchief he began to mimic sadness. He followed by pulling out a dustpan, small whiskbroom, and swept the center of the now empty box.

Going to a nearby large trash container he opened the top, and deposited the make-believe dust. As he walked away he pretended to hear something from the waste receptacle, and walked back to it. Opening it again he examined the inside and after reaching in, coaxed out a bewildered-looking Trevor. The audience went wild with approval.

Amid the riotous applause Trevor walked back to his seat, seemingly disoriented by the experience. Tommy asked," Was there a trapdoor under the box? What did you see?"

"I—I didn't see anything, and it felt like a long time. I mean real long, like a week." His words were uncertain and the smiling youth, who only a short time ago, bathed in the admiration of the audience, now became more reserved, and hesitant.

"I think we'll call it a night and head home," their mother said, after getting up from her seat and moving toward the tent's exit. "It's been a long day, and everyone is tired, including me."

The boys climbed into the back seat of their mom's 1955 black Nash Ambassador. Usually they fought over the front passenger seat. This evening, with its star-studded sky was best viewed from the spacious back seat window; neither boy appeared eager to talk. With arms resting on the rear seat's cushion, they gazed skyward as the night swallowed the car's glowing red taillights.

By the time they reached home the twins were sound asleep, each resting in the hollow of the door's armrest and seat. Ruth prodded her boys awake and into the house, imploring them, "Wash up, and brush your teeth, before getting into bed."

"Goodnight boys, sweet dreams," she called out as she went to her room. Alone with her thoughts, she wondered how, Raymond, her late husband would have handled the situation. *It's tough being a single mom.*

Once inside their bedroom and too tired to talk, the boys quickly succumbed to sleep.

***

.

Jacob's face ached. His tongue tasted blood and stomach burned with want; he made his way north, along the desolate highway. He knew it was too late for anyone to pick up a stranger; especially one that appeared as bedraggled as he was. Staying in the shoulder of the oncoming lane, he could see the telltale lights of an approaching vehicle, fearing the police; he avoided notice by ducking into the brush along road. He was tired, too but wanted distance between him and Sturgeon Bay.

He came upon a fruit stand set back a short distance from the road. It was small, barely eight-feet square. A windowless, securely locked white door stood center, on the side facing the motorway and prevented access. Peering into one of the side windows, Jacob saw vague outlines of jars, presumably holding something to eat. His belly growled.

After circling the red-clapboard shrouded structure, looking for an entry point, he eyed the door again. He remembered that sometimes people concealed the key to a door close by, avoiding the need to carry it around. His fingers began to grope the ledges and sanctuaries of concealments. Something began to crawl on the back of his right hand and it forced him to pull back briefly. Again he slid his hand across the inside board of the overhanging soffit; his finger found a nail. Attached to it swung the elusive key.

Jacob Inserted the key; the lock gave way to his twist and nudge. His hands trembled as he slowly pushed the door inward. The hinges growled, as if to object to being disturbed by this late-night foray. He checked his advance and knew he only needed a modest opening for his thin physique.

Once inside, his hands fondled the neatly positioned jars that lined the interior. It was difficult to know what each container held, concealed in the black and gray shadows. He randomly selected three jars, only taking what he could carry and began to back out. His left arm, the one embracing two of the jars, brushed against something. It was the heart pounding sound of glass shattering that caused Jacob to hold his breath. Silence. With bated breath he waited, avoiding any additional racket from a hasty retreat. Satisfied his accident hadn't alerted anyone nearby, he carefully stepped outside, put his purloined meal on the wood deck, and snapped the lock in place. Not wanting to leave any sign of a break-in, the broken jar, possibly the deed of a foraging rodent. He replaced the key, collected his meals and fled into the forest. Pushing branches aside, Jacob stumbled through the thicket, boring his way into isolation.

***

With school out, Ruth didn't have to prod the twins into action so they would not miss the school bus. After her light breakfast she wrote a short note about what chores she wanted the boys to complete while she was at work. Her expectations were reasonable, making their beds and cleaning up after themselves following meals. Today she added a job that was the least favorite, raking and weeding the garden.

Lying face up and staring at the ceiling, Tommy called out. "Trevor, you up?"

"Uh-huh," he responded half-heartedly and rolled in the direction of Tommy. "Whaddya want?"

"What did you see in that box?"

"I don't know. I was...like sleeping." His response was shaky and hesitant. "What made you try to hold me back?"

"That clown had a funny look, not like Red Skelton funny, just scary funny," Tommy confessed. "Ya know, ever since I put on that thing from Uncle Jonathan's trunk, I feel, and see stuff."

"Do you think we should tell Mom what we did?" Trevor asked, while sitting up and swinging his legs outside the bed.

"No!" We'll get in trouble for doing it." Tommy's disapproval of admitting snooping in their uncle's stuff was instantaneous. "We won't go up there again. Okay?"

"Sure thing, Tom," Trevor backed off, sensing Tommy's uneasiness.

After breakfast the boys cleaned up and went to tend to their chores. The garden was modest in size, but satisfied the needs of Ruth and her boys. She liked to grow strawberries, asparagus, cucumbers, and carrots; all suitable for canning, a hobby she enjoyed. The asparagus and strawberries were her early crop, but the twins' love of strawberries resulted in a somewhat smaller harvest reaching the dinner table.

As the boys weeded the garden their conversation turned to their uncle. "Mom said that Uncle Jonathan would be visiting us next week Sunday." Tommy spoke excitedly, knowing his uncle's visits were always filled with presents and fun things to do.

"Where did Mom say he was coming from?" Trevor asked.

"Someplace near Mexico or in Mexico. I think she said it was about the Oldmecks or Olmecs people. Anyway, it's about some real old people."

"I can't think someone actually gets paid for digging in dirt," Trevor scoffed as he less than eagerly worked his trowel in the garden.

As they were about done for the day they spotted a stranger approaching the house from the tree line. He appeared to be older than the boys, but much younger than their mother.

"Hello," he called out to them as he slowly approached.

"Hi," Tommy replied, somewhat skeptical of anyone appearing out of the woods.

"Hi, my name is Jacob. I'm lost."

Tommy and Trevor closed ranks and began to retreat toward the back door of their house. Once they were on the porch they both appeared a bit more secure, knowing that they could swiftly slip inside if they had to.

"Don't worry, kids, I won't hurt you. I'm lost and need directions to the closest highway," Jacob said, while extending his right hand aloft in a sign of peace.

"Remember that Perry Mason show on Saturday?" Trevor asked Tommy.

"Yeah. Why you ask?"

"Remember that the little boy who let that man in the house, his mother got real mad, and told him to get out?" Trevor quietly explained to Tommy. "I don't think Mom would want this guy around either."

Tommy nodded.

Both boys' backs pressed against the screen door. Each held a garden implement as if it were a lethal weapon. Trevor reached behind and blindly groped for the knob. Pulling the door open he slipped inside, leaving his brother to keep an eye on Jacob. .He headed for the telephone that was mounted on the kitchen wall and called his mother.

"Public library, this is Ruth Roberts. How may I help you," her voice was steady and practiced.

"Mom! There's someone here who's lost. Tommy is outside on the back porch," Trevor rattled off his litany of concerns before his mother blocked the surge.

"Trevor—Trevor," she said in a calming tone, "Slowly and calmly tell me what is happening."

Trevor, taking a deep breath began his story again, only with more control. "This guy came out of the woods and said he was lost. He is kinda dirty and his clothes are torn."

Disturbed by the news, she asked, "Did he try to hurt you?"

"No, we're fine. I thought we should call you." He became more confident hearing his mother's voice.

"Now listen Trevor," she said firmly, "tell Tommy to come in the house, and lock the door. I will call the police, but under no circumstances should either of you leave the house. Understand?"

"Yes Mom," he agreed, hung up the phone and went to retrieve his brother.

***

"Helen, I have a bit of an emergency at home. You'll have to handle it for a while by yourself," Ruth said, as she began to dial the police department. The station was two blocks behind the library, but she did not waste time with a personal visit. After making the call, she hurried to her car, and home.

***

"Mom said get in here," Trevor hollered through the screen door. Taking his brother's words seriously he backed into the house while continuing to hold his trowel in a defensive stance. The screen door slapped shut. The twins pushed the heavy entrance door closed, sealing it with the deadbolt as an additional precaution.

After the boys went inside, Jacob appeared at a loss for action. He looked forlorn and began to aimlessly retreat from the house, following the only gravel road that would take him somewhere. His exit was soon blocked by Ruth Roberts' approaching car.

Jacob halted. Standing in the middle of the road he appeared uncertain what to do next. After she stopped her car, about twenty feet from him,

Ruth exited the Nash, but remained behind the driver's door. "May I help you young man?" Seeing his pitiable state, her voice was gentle and appeared concerned. Before he could answer her first question, she inquired, "What's your name?"

"My name's Jacob Rubenstein. I'm lost." His response was polite and void of any hostility.

Sensing his openness, Ruth continued her calm inquiry. "Where do you live?"

"I'm not from around here. I came from Milwaukee and traveled to Green Bay. A guy told me that I could probably get a job in the orchards around here. I haven't had much luck."

As Jacob finished his brief summary, Sheriff Collins' squad car grumbled over the loose gravel, and came to a stop behind the black Nash. Getting out, the sheriff walked toward Ruth, his demeanor sober. He paused next to her, meeting her gaze face-to-face, his blue eyes revealing sincere concern for her safety. "Everything okay Mrs. Roberts? Is he giving you any trouble?" he asked, while adjusting his utility belt and holstered gun.

"No trouble. I left work when the boys told me he was on the property. His name is Jacob. I think he may be a runaway from home. He said he was looking for work." Ruth's words to the sheriff were hushed. "Be gentle with him, Bob. I think he had a few tough breaks."

Leaving her by the car, Sheriff Collins approached Jacob, and said, "Why don't you come with me, son. I have to take you into town, and see what we can do for you." His method was peaceful, knowing that every drifter wasn't necessarily trouble; each one had to be humanely dealt with.

As the two of them passed Ruth on their way to the squad car, she gave Jacob a sympathetic smile. He briefly returned her smile, and then resumed a distrustful attitude.

Once the sheriff departed for town, Ruth went to the house to check on the boys. Finding them safe, she instructed them to shower after their work in the garden and change into some clean clothes. She also told them to stay close to the house, and she would bring home a meal for supper.

Before going back to work she made a visit to the sheriff's office. "Hi, Bob. How is Jacob doing?"

"Just fine. I'll keep him locked up for the night. I'll give him a meal, run some inquires making sure he didn't commit any crime, and send him on his way tomorrow."

"Bob, he looks like he could use some clothes, too. If it's all right with you, I'll check with Father Sebastian to see what he has in the Saint Vincent bin?"

"Sure thing, Ruth. Gary Simons is on tonight, and I will let him know that you'll be back," Sheriff Collins said. He rose from his wooden swivel chair and escorted Ruth to the door.

"Goodbye, Bob and thanks again for coming out to the house," Ruth said, retreating outside, setting a course for the Stella Maris Parish, and Father Sebastian's rectory.

***

The boys helped set the table while their mom busied herself transferring the carryout food onto serving dishes. It was Tommy's turn to lead in saying grace. After he finished, Ruth began the dinner conversation.

"It looks like you boys did a super job in the garden." She always gave Tommy, and Trevor jobs because she believed in the adage that "Idle hands are the Devil's tools."

"Thanks, Mom," they said, almost in unison.

"What's going to happen to that guy?" Tommy asked.

"His name is Jacob. He seems to have had some bad luck. He needs a place to sleep and a meal."

"Did Sheriff Collins throw him in jail, Mom?" Trevor asked, excitedly.

"Sheriff Collins did not throw him in jail," she answered, visibly annoyed by his tone. "He simply let Jacob sleep in one of the empty cells. I also visited Father Sebastian and got clothing for him from the Saint Vincent donation box."

"You went into the jail?" Trevor exclaimed.

"I wasn't *in jail*. I dropped off some clothes, to give to Jacob." Exasperated with the Trevor's focus, she changed the topic.

Ruth was excited about the upcoming trip by her brother Jonathan, which was enthusiastically shared by Tommy, and Trevor. Because of his arrival, she told the boys of her expectations from them, and gave specific instructions of what each one was required to do.

After dinner, the usual routine of cleaning up was followed by a night of viewing television. It being summer vacation, the boys enjoyed an additional hour of TV, before going to bed at nine. Their mother's programing choice on Wednesday was *The Lawrence Welk's Show*, followed by *The Adventures of Ozzie and Harriet*. Both of the shows were of no interest to the boys, so they went to their room early.

The boys changed into pajamas, and rested on their beds. Tommy started to read a book when Trevor asked him, "Did you see any more ghosts?" His question did not have a mocking tone.

"When that guy came out of the woods, I thought it might be one, but you saw him, too. No, only on the beach." He answered reflectively, adding, "Oh, outside my window too, but maybe it was a dream, like Mom said."

Neither one spoke the rest of the night; sleep claiming each before they could brush their teeth. Ruth Roberts checked in on them, shut off the reading lights, turned on the night light, and retired for the evening. She did not notice Mister Devlin standing outside, beyond the reach of the room's glow.

***

"Good morning, Sheriff. What brings you to the library today—official business?" Ruth chimed, as Sheriff Collins advanced toward the library's checkout desk.

"Sort of," he replied cheerfully. "I have some news that may please you." After leaning on Ruth's elevated desk with both his arms, he began to quietly inform her of his activities concerning Jacob. His account produced a smile that brightened into a full grin.

"After you dropped off the clothes for Jacob, Father Sebastian made a visit to the jail and had a talk with him. His assessment was that the kid had a few unfortunate starts, and needed a leg up. Making a few calls on his behalf, Father was able to get Jacob some seasonal work. It's temporary, but at least he will have employment and a place to stay."

"A place to stay?"

"Yep, the job at Cherry Hill Orchards came with a bed in their hired hands' bunkhouse. Nothing fancy, but clean and dry. And by the looks of Jacob, something that he has needed for some time." The sheriff finished relaying the good news, and then excused himself, saying, "Have to run. I thought you would like to know."

Delighted by the news she returned to her work. Her reverie was broken by the sound of the telephone. Ruth answered in her customary scripted response, "Public library, this is Ruth Roberts. How may I help you?"

It was her brother Jonathan, and after hearing his news, she was certain the day couldn't get any better.

**

Once everyone was seated, and grace said, Ruth began telling Tommy and Trevor the news she could hardly contain. "Uncle Jonathan will not be coming here as planned."

Both boys stopped eating, and shot glances at their mother in disbelief. "But Uncle Jonathan said he was coming here!" Tommy howled.

"Why not!" Trevor chorused over Tommy's protest.

"Calm down, boys," Ruth interjected. "He isn't coming here because we are going to visit him at his work in the Milwaukee Natural History Museum."

"Wow!" Trevor exclaimed.

To which Tommy excitedly asked," When are we going?

"Well, I took two days off from work. Helen said she could easily handle the library for a couple of days. Since the library is closed this Monday, I will have four days off—we leave tomorrow!"

After running through the list of things to bring on the trip, she emphasized a few essentials. "Don't forget to bring Sunday church clothes, underwear, and your tooth brushes."

"Where are we going to stay?" Trevor asked.

"Because your uncle is single, and lives in a small apartment, he is treating us to a two-night stay at the Schroeder Hotel."

"A trip to Milwaukee, and a hotel, too!" Trevor said, barely containing his excitement.

"We'll watch *Zorro* after you pack your bags, and then it is bedtime. We are getting an early start. I hope to leave here by *five*," Ruth said, emphasizing the time.

Tommy and Trevor helped clean up, and quickly went to pack. The boys each had a small suitcase sufficiently sized to accommodate their needs. After hurriedly packing, they sat on the living room rug, leaning against the sofa, waiting for their mother to join them.

The name of the *Zorro* episode was, "The Eagle Leaves the Nest." It didn't excite either of the boys as the previous shows. One part did draw comment; when Zorro's deaf-mute Bernardo caused a diversion by using a dry gourd to produce a ghostlike sound.

"That sounded like you Tommy when we were in the at…" Trevor checked his comment, and glanced at his mother to see if she heard. Ruth appeared to be nodding off, and his remark escaped her notice.

"I think we should go to bed. Mom looks tired, and we have to get up early," Tommy said. After getting up from the floor, both boys gave their mom a kiss on the cheek, and went off to bed. Ruth followed their lead by turning off the television, securing the house for the night, and retiring to her bedroom.

***

It was the usual pandemonium; the twins fighting over who goes first in the bathroom, and who will sit in the front seat of the car. At five o'clock the dawning sun was already hanging above the horizon. A slight lake breeze filled the air, causing everybody to throw on a light jacket to shield them from the morning chill. Once everyone was in place, Ruth placed the car in gear, and aimed the Nash south, toward their destination.

The four-hour drive was without incident. Ruth stopped twice, once for breakfast in Sturgeon Bay and the other for lunch in Sheboygan. The battle over the front sent ended when both boys decided to take a nap in the back. When they arrived in Milwaukee, Ruth was tired, and looked forward to taking a catnap before going out to dinner that night.

***

Ruth parked her car on a side street, near the museum, and cautioned Tommy and Trevor. "Stay close to me and don't wander off. This is the *big city* and things can happen."

Ignoring her words, the twins outpaced her and briskly scrambled up the impressive stone stairs. Having reached the museum's front entrance they urged her to hurry. "C'mon, Mom," Trevor called.

"Stay right there. Uncle Jonathan isn't going anywhere, and neither are you two if you don't settle down."

No sooner did their mother reach the doorway, than the boys bolted through the massive entryway and stood motionless in amazement at the interior. Standing in the center of an ornate floor mosaic, Tommy and Trevor's heads swiveled around, attempting to take in the entire scene. Three towering floors, joined by two bordering sets of marble enclosed staircases, surrounded them. On their left, a wide entryway into the display area, beyond the stairwell, beckoned the curious.

"Not now, boys. We first have to go upstairs," Ruth said, as she nudged them along toward the elevator.

The elevator operator delivered them to the fourth floor, a floor off-limits to the general public, and guided them to her brother's office. "Doctor Morrison's office is down that hallway; the second door on the right."

Having heard the clamor of the boys, Jonathan walked into the passageway to greet them. Tall and ruddy, with sun-bleached hair, he moved enthusiastically in their direction. "You boys are growing like bamboo," he said. After scuffing each one's hair he embraced his sister, giving her a kiss on the cheek.

"You look as beautiful as ever. How was the ride?"

"Well, it's not something I would care to do on a regular basis, but it wasn't too bad. I could use a little rest. Do you suppose I could leave Tommy and Trevor with you while I go to the hotel for a little nap?"

"Sure thing. As a matter of fact, I was going to suggest that myself. You know where it is. Everything has been taken care of; just give your name at the desk. I'll put these boys to work cleaning off dinosaur bones," he quipped.

The twins were full of questions. "What is an archeologist? Trevor asked."

"An archeologist is a person who digs up things left behind by past civilizations. We collect artifacts, label what we find, and study them. In a way, we are garbage pickers of the past," he joked.

While moving through the labyrinth of display cases within the museum, wood flooring groaned underfoot, providing a mysterious ambiance to the tour. The exhibition rooms included lifelike panoramas of historical and geological occurrences. One of the displays was that of an active volcano flow, with pulsing red ribbons of lava, mesmerizing the boys into silence.

Later in the tour, something Tommy and Trevor saw struck them with unease. There, inside a glass enclosed case was a helmet mask, similar to the one in their attic. They exchanged uncomfortable glances, knowing they had violated their uncle's privacy when they went into his trunk.

"What's that, Uncle Jonathan?" Tommy uneasily asked.

"That?" he pointed to the discombobulated confluence of antelope horns, crocodile jaws, and wart hog tusks. "That's a Wabele mask. It is used by a highly secret society of Sierra Leone, called the Poro Society. It is used in one of their rituals to contact the dead."

***

Jacob approached the Roberts' house on a bicycle borrowed from the owner of the Cherry Hill Orchard. He appeared quite different from the last time he traveled this road. A used pair of jeans, sweatshirt, and light jacket now covered his lean frame, but he was clean. To him, they seemed new by comparison to the tattered apparel he wore only a couple of days ago. Fighting the irregular surface of the driveway, his steering had a slight wobble.

The purpose of this trip was to thank Mrs. Roberts for all the kindness shown to him, and her part in finding him shelter and employment. As he neared the backside of the building he noticed some movement to his left, opposite the driveway's side of the house.

"Mrs. Roberts!" he called, assuming the elusive figure was that of his advocate. "Mrs. Roberts!" he shouted again, while approaching the corner of the dwelling where he thought she'd disappeared.

Carefully resting his borrowed bike alongside a birch tree, he went toward the corner of the building. When that side of the structure was in full view, he saw something that made his heart pound and hands perspire.

"What are you doing here?" Jacob challenged the presence of a clown, who only a week ago, was responsible for a beating he received at the circus. The makeup-laden comic turned toward Jacob and began to advance. Jacob retreated a few steps, his eyes darting from side to side, looking for some type of weapon.

A razorback bow rake rested against the siding of the house and within reach. Jacob grabbed the handle of the rake, holding the tines toward the clown, who continued to advance; unbothered by Jacob's unconvincing bearing of strength. Moist hands nervously gripped the wood handle, waiting for the clown's next move.

With white-gloved hands raised menacingly toward Jacob, the clown lunged forward, grabbed the business end of the rake, and yanked it from him. Agilely spinning it around like a baton, the teeth of the garden implement now became the instrument of pain. The clown repeatedly struck Jacob, over and over again, furrowing his flesh with ribbons of blood. He beat him into unconsciousness. Even then, the blows continued.

***

After Sunday Mass, Uncle Jonathan treated his sister and two nephews to brunch before their trip back to Door County. He also took the wheel of the Nash, which she willingly gave up, saying, "Now I can keep a close eye those two troublemakers in back." Her remark caused both boys to respond with snickers.

"I could use a couple of weeks with you after spending a month in a Guatemalan jungle." Jonathan broke through the laughter coming from the rear seat. "When construction on the new museum begins in a couple of years, my work in Guatemala will be an important addition to its collection of Maya artifacts."

"Does that mean you will be spending more time in Wisconsin?" Ruth asked.

"Initially? No. I have to go back several times to secure more objects for the display panoramas and shoot more photographs. We want the museum experience to be more lifelike. Besides the usual glass-enclosed display cases, we are going to create a tropical rainforest. Visitors will travel through the exhibit, complete with jungle sounds."

"Can we go in the jungle, too, Uncle Jonathan?" Trevor spoke up.

"You bet you can. I will give you a personal tour as soon as it's done," he said while glancing in the rearview mirror at the twins. Their smiles produced a like response on Jonathan's face.

Having gone almost nonstop visiting the museum, the art museum, and finally a Saturday night movie, Tommy, and Trevor dozed off. Once Ruth was certain the boys were fast asleep, she began her narrative of the two previous weeks and the death of the lighthouse keeper's daughter.

Having listened to her story, he asked, "How are the boys dealing with this?"

"I'm a little concerned with Tommy. At one point he claimed he saw the ghost of Angelica."

"These tragic events can trigger neurosis at a young age. It can be more significant when the death is someone known to the person. Maybe I can have a talk with Tommy when the moment is right?" Jonathan said, appearing concerned.

"Yes, I think it will be helpful."

Ruth stirred the boys awake when they reached Sturgeon Bay. Jonathan insisted on buying dinner. It was the beginning of tourist season, so there were plenty of restaurants from which to choose.

While Ruth and Jonathan debated dining choices, a collective request came from the twins, "Pizza!"

***

They left the restaurant, content with their meal. Worn-out from the trip, plus full stomachs, the boys lazily resumed their rear seat positions. It was the day after the summer solstice, leaving them with nearly three hours of daylight.

Ruth assumed the driver's seat on the final leg of the trip. She behaved like a tour guide, pointing out any changes to the county since her brother's last visit. Although, little physically changed from nine months ago, but the people did. Marriages, deaths, and births, all the usual happenings in life, but in a small town, they loomed large.

She turned her car into the driveway and stopped a couple of feet beyond the roadside mailbox. Leaving the car run, she retrieved two-day's worth of mail. She briefly scanned the contents, then placed the assortment of envelopes on the dash and drove her car to within a few feet of the garage.

Both rear doors sprung open. Tommy and Trevor headed for the house.

"Not so fast you two. Get back here and lend a hand," Ruth sternly commanded.

As the boys turned toward their mother, Trevor noticed a bike leaning against a nearby tree. Curious, he walked over to it. "Hey! Mom, someone left a bike on our lawn."

Baffled by its presence, everyone converged on the bicycle. It was then that Jonathan noticed the body sprawled on the ground.

"Ruth! Keep the boys there," Jonathan ordered in such an unusual tone, that she shot a probing look in his direction. Her glance moved from her brother to the side of the house. Observing the crumpled form, she forcibly gathered her boys and herded them in. Once inside, she demanded them to stay-put, and went back outside to join her brother.

"Oh! My God! It's that young man I told you about," she exclaimed upon reaching Jonathan's side. "Is he dead?" Her voice trembled in shock at the sight of Jacob's battered and bloody body.

"Yes. I'm no coroner, but this boy had been beaten to death. And that rake would appear to be the weapon." He pointed to the blood-covered object a few feet from them. "I also think it wasn't too long ago, either. Call the police now!" he ordered. "Where are the boys?"

"Inside, I didn't want them to see this," she said, as they moved back toward the rear entrance to the house.

"The killer, or killers, could be inside," Jonathan said, as he quickened his pace. Ruth ran in tandem behind her brother.

Jonathan flung the door open so hard that it bounced off the doorstop set into the floor, the recoil of which almost stuck him in the face.

"Tommy! Trevor! Where are you?" Ruth yelled.

Puzzled by the alarm in their mother's voice, the twins appeared in the living room doorway. "Here we are," Tommy said, puzzled by her urgency. "What do you want?"

"I want you two to stay right here in the kitchen," she demanded, lacking her usual calm.

"Hurry Ruth, make the call. Where do you keep your kitchen knives?"

While picking up the phone's receiver, Ruth pointed to a kitchen drawer near the sink. He followed her direction, selected a large utility knife, and hurried into the interior of the house. Cautiously searching for any would-be assailant, he flipped on the wall switches and lamps, illuminating every recess. Soon the building was emblazoned in light.

Meanwhile, Ruth called the sheriff's office. Listening to their mother talk, Tommy and Trevor became aware of the seriousness of the situation.

Trevor leaned over in his kitchen chair, and whispered to Tommy, who sat in a seat next to him, "Someone is dead outside." His brother remained silent and glanced uncomfortably at the bolted kitchen door.

"All clear!" Jonathan exclaimed as he entered the kitchen's foyer.

"The sheriff will be here shortly," Ruth reported. "Did you check the attic?"

"No, I didn't. I'll check it now."

Jonathan disappeared from the hallway and moved to the back of the house, where the stairwell to the top story was located. Carefully opening the door, he turned on the passageway light, peered to his right, beyond the doorframe, and up the incline of steps. He felt a slight breeze against his neck; it came from the partially opened window on his left. He turned, faced the window and with the knife free hand, pulled the lower sash down.

He refocused his attention on the solitary bare bulb. It was suspended from a length of wire connected to the junction box. Fixed to an unadorned joist, its glow revealed partially finished walls leading up to the exposed skeleton of rafters and roofing boards.

He kept the kitchen knife blade pointing in front of him and slowly edged upwards. With every forward movement the steps groaned under his weight, which betrayed any hope of surprising an interloper. Now eye-level with the floor, he uneasily scanned the attic. An assortment of boxes and trunks provided cover to any possible intruder. The plastic-encapsulated clothing, which hung from improvised poles set among the beams, resembled human forms. Long shadows, products of the falling sun, cast menacing shapes, making every nook and cranny appear unfriendly.

As Jonathan began to step onto the attic's floor he heard the approaching wail of a siren. Having thought better of the idea to confront any intruder alone, he quickly turned and hurried down the stairs.

Ruth rushed outside after hearing the sound of the advancing squad car. Jonathan followed her. Meeting Sheriff Collins, Ruth said, "The body is over there." She pointed to the far side of the house. The trio moved in unison to the spot. While walking, she said, "Do you remember my brother Jonathan?"

"Oh, sure I do. Doctor Morrison, I wish it were under better circumstances that we meet again," he said, forcing a slight smile and extending his hand in greeting.

"Yes, I agree," he said, accepting the sheriff's handshake. "But, Jonathan will do fine. I'm not one for titles."

The sound of another approaching squad car added to the already tension filled air. "That will be Deputy Williams," the sheriff remarked. "He was in Fish Creek, when you called. I also automatically contacted Sturgeon Bay for an ambulance. I was unsure of the victim's condition. They'll be here shortly."

"Poor kid," Sheriff Collins, said remorsefully. "Why was he here?"

"I don't know. We returned from Milwaukee when Trevor noticed the cycle on our lawn," Ruth said, pointing toward the bike propped against a tree.

"Any sign of forced entry into your house, Ruth?"

"No, not that I know of," she answered the sheriff hesitantly.

Jonathan interrupted. "I found the rear window opened at the base of the stairs leading to the attic, But it wasn't forced."

"Are you certain no one is in your house?" Collins asked.

"I checked the lower part of the house and was starting to explore the second floor, when you came."

"That was risky," said Collins, giving Jonathan a look of disapproval. "Show me the way to the attic."

Jonathan led him to the attic's entrance, opened the door, and stood back to allow the sheriff to pass.

"Sheriff!" Jonathan called out, before the sheriff could take another step.

"What is it?" he asked, while drawing his sidearm.

"That window on your left was opened when I first got here. I closed it before I went upstairs. See, it's opened now."

"Hurry, go tell my deputy, and get back in the kitchen until I give the all clear." After giving those orders he moved cautiously up the stairs, with his revolver pointing the way.

As soon as Deputy Williams received the information from Jonathan, he quickly, but silently moved to the front of the house. Drawing his weapon, too, he approached the opened window. Nothing stirred in the vicinity of the building, or beyond the trees outside the picket fence and along the highway. When he approached the window, he noticed evidence of someone's recent presence by the matted down grass below the rear window. The shoe impressions were unusually large. He held his position and waited.

Meanwhile the sheriff reached the top of the stairwell and guardedly moved into the center of the attic. On each end of the top floor the facing colonial, double hung windows, remained closed. The reflected image of Sheriff Collins played within the rectangular glass grids of the windowpanes. The light from his flashlight flickered back as its beam explored the edges of the casements.

He moved further in to his left and spotted an open trunk with a white sheet haphazardly lying in front of it. The insides appeared rifled, but uncertain of the contents, he could not determine if anything was missing. Making a final sweep of the interior, he retreated downstairs. He stopped at the bottom window. Leaning out over the windowsill he told his deputy to meet him back in the kitchen.

"No one is hiding in the attic, but I did see that a trunk was opened and rummaged through," the sheriff commented, as he entered the kitchen. "Was that done by anyone here?"

Meeting each other's eyes, the twins displayed the look of guilt but said nothing.

Ruth Roberts could sense some culpability from them and sternly asked, "Did you boys go in Uncle Jonathan's things? This is a serious matter, and you both better tell us all you know."

Neither of the twins ever saw their mother so furious. Her stern demand made Tommy and Trevor compete for the telling of their involvement.

"Tommy—" Trevor began only to be cut off by his brother.

"Trevor said, we should—" Tommy fought back.

"Stop!" their mother demanded, her nerves already frayed because of the murder "Trevor, you go first. Tell us everything you know."

Sheriff Collins seated himself at the kitchen table and removed a notebook from his rear pocket. "Go ahead, tell all of us what you know," he said, and pulled a pen from his breast pocket.

Trevor's story was exactly the same as his brother's version, except both boys blamed each other for the idea to snoop in their uncle's trunk. When done, both swore that they put everything back the way it was and shut the chest.

"When I looked into the opened trunk, I didn't see the mask that you boys described," the sheriff said. "Jonathan, would you please accompany me to the attic again, and we will both have another look?"

Ruth remained in the kitchen, with Deputy Williams and the twins, glaring at her boys in disapproval. Tommy and Trevor remained mute, avoiding eye contact with their mother. To the boys, the absence of their uncle and the sheriff seemed like an eternity as they squirmed uneasily in their chairs. No sooner had their uncle returned, breaking the tenseness in the kitchen, when the sound of an approaching siren rekindled the uneasiness within the room.

"Well, it would appear the Wabele mask was stolen," their uncle declared.

"Doctor Morrison—I mean, Jonathan, will you please come to my office tomorrow?" Sheriff Collins asked. "Actually, I think everyone should come. I will need to get fingerprint samples for comparison purposes.

Let's say, around ten?" Jonathan pensively nodded in agreement.

"Sure," Ruth said, appearing bewildered by all the upheaval she was suddenly thrust into.

"In the meantime, your house is officially a crime scene and the area where the body was found will be roped off before we leave—no one should go near that spot, or in the attic. Also, Deputy Williams will remain here for the night. He just came on duty, so he's rested enough for a night stakeout. Considering the seriousness of the crime, I would prefer you stay in town, but with the tourist season, I doubt you could find a vacancy for everyone."

"Actually, Bob, I was going to ask you that favor," Ruth said, blushing slightly from her slip of familiarity, calling him by his first name in front of her brother. "Having someone guarding us tonight will be a great relief."

"No problem," he said, somberly. "I will need to get the fingerprint kit out of my car and see if I can lift any prints from that window or trunk. Once I'm done with that and the outside area is secure, I will make certain your doors and windows are locked, too. After that, I'll be on my way."

Ruth and Jonathan retrieved the rest of their belongings from the Nash, and then supervised the boys as they prepared for bed. Once everybody was in place for the night, Jonathan made a final sweep of the house, and then retired to his room. As a further precaution, he left his door opened slightly, so he would be able to hear any strange sounds which may break his slumber. A baseball bat rested alongside his bed, within reach, as an additional safeguard.

Sleep did not come easily despite the long tiring trip. After tossing and turning, eventually slumber overcame everyone, except for Deputy Williams, who struggled to stay awake as he sat in his squad car. The fleeting image of Mister Devlin's reflection in the officer's rearview mirror went unnoticed by him.

***

The household stirred to life and its occupants gradually converged on the kitchen. Drawn to the smell of fresh coffee and bacon, Jonathan wearing a reddish plaid robe over his blue pajamas, greeted his sister, "Boy that sure smells good, Sis. A bit chilly this morning, isn't it?" he added.

Ruth did not answer immediately "I don't think I got more than two hours of sleep last night, knowing our house was the scene of a murder," Ruth lamented. "Remember, I met that kid when he was alive. Seeing Jacob's body like that is very troubling.

Jonathan did not answer, unsure of what to say.

"I'm sorry Jonathan, my mind is on yesterday. By noon all you need are shorts and a T-shirt this time of year," she said half-heartedly, as she poured hot coffee into his cup.

"Ruth, why don't you pour another cup and I'll take it out to the deputy. I'm sure he would appreciate it," Jonathan said, eager to go outside. She sluggishly obliged.

He unlatched the door and carefully maneuvered his way to the parked squad. As he approached the car he noticed the driver's side door ajar. He also saw the police officer was absent. After cautiously placing the cup on the top of the car's hood, he scanned the area and began to walk toward the tree line of the adjoining forest.

"Deputy Williams!" he called out. His call went unanswered. Glancing down, Jonathan noticed the matted down trail through the dew-laden grass. He followed it until it terminated at the woods. Continuing ten feet beyond the thicket's border he found the officer lying with what appeared to be a large white scarf coiled around his neck. Going to the body, Jonathan placed his hand on Deputy Williams' jugular, searching for a pulse. He found none. He rose quickly from his crouched position and nervously scanned the surroundings. Panicked by the death and not knowing what may still be out there, he made a dash for the house.

As he bounced through the entrance doorway, Jonathan gasped, "Call the sheriff! Now! Deputy Williams is dead!"

The abruptness of the announcement caught everyone by surprise. The twins and Ruth, frozen by the revelation, tried to process what they had heard. Regaining her focus, Ruth ripped the phone from its wall cradle and with a trembling hand dialed. Gary Simons answered her call.

"Gary, Deputy Williams is dead!" Her words ran in panic. On the other end, Deputy Simons told Ruth since Williams had not made his routine call; the sheriff was already on his way. After, she hung up and sat down, afraid her wobbling legs would not support her.

Outside, a cacophony of sirens converged on the Robert's household. Inside, an unfamiliar silence held everyone in suspense, uncertain what to make of the recent event.

Jonathan broke the concentrated silence and gently said, "Ruth, stay here with Tommy and Trevor. I'll meet with Sheriff Collins." He rose from his chair and gently touched her back as he made his way toward the outside door.

Jonathan emerged from the house and waved to the sheriff, meeting him, as he exited the squad. "He's over there," he said, motioning toward the tree line. A column of police vehicles also came to a stop behind the sheriff's car; a nearby community's police car, an ambulance, and a Wisconsin State Trooper's patrol car.

They stopped and the edge of the woods. Sheriff Collins said, "Please stay here. I don't want the crime scene to be further compromised." Jonathan nodded and stepped back a few paces. The sheriff then gingerly picked his way through the underbrush.

He gave the area a quick going over, then rejoined Ruth's brother and the two of them moved slowly back to the house. Neither of them spoke. Jonathan looked bewildered and offered the only solace he could. "I'm sorry for your loss, sheriff."

"Thank you," he said, his eyes pooled with tears. Sheriff Collins then picked up the pace and with a determined gait, closed on the collection of law enforcement personnel.

When he reached the assembly of police and ambulance staff, he spoke softly. "I'll need to take some pictures before the body can be moved. Also, I will contact the crime lab in Madison for some assistance." Looking at Jonathan, he mechanically said, "I will need a statement from you, too." The sheriff, his eyes still glossy, moved toward his own vehicle to retrieve the camera.

After photographing the crime scene, he called the crime lab, and took Jonathan's statement. The sheriff then sat at the kitchen table. He slouched forward with his arms resting on the table, and let out a long sigh. "Ruth I want to talk to the boys again. I feel they know more about this case than they realize." He looked at Ruth and Jonathan then continued. "You both can be in the room, but will have to sit behind them. I will interview them one at a time. I don't want the boys to have any opportunity to compare stories. And at no time should you offer any opinion, or prompt them. They must say everything they know without any outside influence. Okay?"

"Okay," Ruth agreed. "I sent the boys to their room. I didn't want them to hear or see too much, considering the gravity of the situation. I'll get them."

She returned to the kitchen with the Trevor in tow. Ruth had him sit, on the side of the table, but angled toward Sheriff Collins at the head. Ruth and Jonathan then took their places several feet behind him on the far side of the room. Ruth nodded to the sheriff.

"Well Trevor, I'm going to ask you some questions and I want you to answer truthfully. Okay?"

Trevor nodded timidly.

"There is something about that trunk and the headpiece that you are not telling us. I want you to tell me what you did from the very first time you opened it, until you went downstairs."

Trevor told his story, but added something that was not mentioned in the previous interview. "When Tommy put on that thing and acted like a ghost we both felt a funny chill in the attic."

"A chill? What kind of chill?"

"Like winter, but shorter," Trevor explained.

"Was that the only time you felt the cold?"

He nodded.

"Did you ever go back upstairs after that?"

"Un-uh," Trevor said, vigorously shaking his head.

The sheriff asked slowly and deliberately "Did you see anyone around the house when you went outside or anything strange?"

Trevor began to turn his head around, appearing to search for guidance from his mother.

"Trevor! Look at me," the sheriff said sternly. "You saw something strange? What did you see?"

After a short hesitation Trevor slowly began and then gushed forth a flood of words, "Tommy...said he saw ghosts, or dead people. Even Angelica, by the lighthouse, and outside our bedroom window. He even said that the clown at the circus was evil looking." He squirmed self-consciously in place.

Dumbfounded by the seemingly illogical testimony, Sheriff Collins fought to contain his surprise and amusement. He probed Ruth for guidance, unsure of the validity of the tale, she awkwardly nodded back.

"Tommy saw ghosts?" Sheriff Collins asked, dubiously.

"Yes," she replied, visibly uncomfortable with both the question and her answer.

Suspecting him to be approaching his limit, the sheriff said, "I think I have enough information for now, Trevor. Ruth, would you please get Tommy."

Trevor, anxious to leave, began to accompany his mother, but Sheriff Collins gently halted him. "Why don't you stay here Trevor, until Tommy comes into the kitchen?"

"Okay," he submissively agreed.

When Tommy entered the room, he eyed his brother warily as Trevor departed for their bedroom.

Sheriff Collins repeated all the same questions he asked Trevor, but when it came to the subject of ghosts, he became more direct. "Did you ever see ghosts before you went up in the attic, Tommy?"

"No, sir! Never."

"What about the clown? Why did Trevor say you thought the clown at the circus looked evil?"

"I dunno. He had a scary look."

"You know, Tommy..." the sheriff paused, looked up at the ceiling, as if to search for the rest of his words, and said, "I think that clowns have a scary look, too."

"Oh, no! He was really, really bad looking. He had this funny look. Not funny like the clowns on the TV, but spooky funny." Trevor became visibly disturbed by the question. Ruth also appeared anxious, but she honored her promise of not interrupting and remained silent.

Sensing his reluctance to continue, the sheriff said, "I think I have everything. You can go back to your bedroom, Tommy."

After he departed, Sheriff Collins asked, "What do either of you think? Does Tommy have an emotional problem, or is there any truth to what he said?"

"Sheriff," Jonathan spoke up. "I am somewhat familiar with the superstitions and rites of the Wabele society. This may sound strange to you and illogical, but that missing zoomorphic mask may be the key to both of the murders." As the sheriff was about to say something, he held up his hand to silence any interruption and said, "Please let me finish."

"We are rational people and what I am about to say will not make any sense. As I listened to my nephew explain his story, I was struck by the correlation of events since he put on that headpiece and the misfortune that followed.

"By itself, placing the helmet-mask on would do nothing, but as soon as Tommy donned a cotton sheet *and the Wabele mask*, it changed the equation. The mask and cotton sheet are an integral part of the burial ceremonies. It is like having gasoline and a match; it's explosive. In the Poro Society the mask unlocks dangerous forces, giving the wearer supernatural powers. Uncontrolled, or improperly summoned, these forces can bring havoc into a society, in this case, Door County. My guess, something of immense evil was dormant, and unknowingly, Tommy's actions brought it to life, so to speak. It may be pre-Columbian, or an early pioneer settlement issue, but regardless, something very bad is at its core."

Sheriff Collins rubbed the back of his neck with his right hand and appeared somewhat bewildered. "Jonathan, I'm sure that kind of stuff may be true in West Africa, but I doubt it has any relevance here. Besides, I don't have any suspects from Africa and there isn't any common thread in all the incidents. Angelica's death was an accident,

Jacob was beaten to death and Deputy Williams strangled; perhaps two of them are related, but not all three."

"Sheriff, would you do me a favor?" Jonathan pleaded.

"If I can. Sure, what can I do for you?"

"Call it intuition, but I think you should contact the circus in Stevens Point. Ask them about the clown that Tommy said was evil looking. The reason I say that is because it would seem Tommy has a special gift in detecting spirits and negative forces." Jonathan rose from his chair and moved closer to the sheriff, who was already standing. "I'm willing to bet," Jonathan said, "that the clown skipped his act and is no longer there."

"Sure, I can do that, if you think he is in some way connected to all this," the sheriff said. "Based on what I find, I will either be able to scratch a suspect from my list, or add one."

***

With dinner over, the boys hurried into the living room to watch television, leaving Ruth alone with her brother.

"Jonathan, would you mind taking me to work tomorrow?" she asked as the two of them cleared the kitchen table. "I don't want the boys to be left alone, even with the increased police surveillance. They will have to come, too." Her voice strained with the combination of pleading, concern, and exhaustion.

"You bet, Sis," he said compassionately. "I was going to suggest that. I think it will be good for everyone to get away from this house for a while."

The unexpected ringing of the telephone broke the reflective mood causing Ruth to flinch. She moved briskly, pulling the handset from its wall mount, before a second ring could sound. "Hello," she whispered, apprehensively. After listening in silence for a moment, she said, "Sure thing, sheriff. He's right here."

Jonathan reached out and took the phone from Ruth. "Hi, sheriff, what can I do for you?"

He remained silent as he held the telephone receiver to his ear, while leaning against the wall. His expression slowly changed from puzzlement to worry. Finally, the one sided conversation ended when he said, "Yes, I will and thank you for informing me."

He returned the phone to its mount and looked at Ruth. "The sheriff wants me to stop in at his office tomorrow. It would appear the clown from the circus you and the boys went to, has something to do with the murders." He paused, took a seat at the table and continued. "The sheriff was able to contact the circus manager as they were in the process of packing up and getting ready to move to the next town. The odd thing was the clown; Mister Devlin, left abruptly, never gave notice, or even picked up his payroll check. The sheriff wants to talk to me alone. Do you suppose the boys could stay with you at the library during my visit with him?"

"Sure, it won't be the first time," Ruth said, visibly showing signs of apprehension. "What do you think this means—I mean regarding our safety?"

"I think we must be extra careful. And by that, we need to keep a watchful eye and never let the twins out of sight," Jonathan firmly warned.

Ruth nodded meditatively.

***

Jonathan opted to walk the two blocks to the sheriff's office, leaving his sister's car in the library's parking lot. The front of the building was lined with three vehicles; a Ford black and gray Wisconsin State Patrol car, a gray Edsel Roundup crime-lab van marked *Coroner*, and a black 1957 Cadillac Fleetwood hearse.

It was obvious to Jonathan that his entry into the front office was in the middle of a briefing. Regardless of the interruption, Sheriff Collins extended a warm greeting and introduced Jonathan to the coroner and crime lab's representative. He resumed his thread; "Based on the suspiciously abrupt departure of Mister Devlin, the investigation will be focused on him, for now." Sheriff Collins appeared resolute and confident. "The only material evidence we have is the white scarf found at the last murder scene." Pausing briefly, he looked at the crime lab's rep and said, "I was hoping your laboratory people could come up with something regarding that."

After the meeting Jonathan and Sheriff Collins moved to the back office where they could be alone. "I didn't say anything about the Wabele during the briefing because I don't think they would take it seriously. Actually, I'm having some reservations, too. But I will give you the benefit of the doubt." His tone was conciliatory. "Perhaps your speculation may be more psychosomatic, or generated through suggestive hypnosis, but some aspect of it may have a kernel of truth."

"Sheriff, like I said, I'm only telling you the facts based on the practices of the Poro Society. I too, don't believe, but if someone shares in that belief, who's to say what they can do, or not do." Regarding him with great concern over any outright dismissal of his theory, Jonathan added, "But any exclusion of the possibilities could prove deadly."

"You're right, that's why I wanted to talk with you this morning—let's keep this between us for now. Okay?" Sheriff Collins said, trying not to appear too overbearing.

"Sure thing," Jonathan tersely replied. Frustrated, he continued, "If you will excuse me I think the boys would like some time with their uncle."

Jonathan's walk back to the library was brisk and more determined.

His arrival at the library resulted in a chain reaction—Ruth happy to see her brother and the twins eager to get outside. The boys, impatient for some kind of adventure with their uncle were disappointed to hear, "Before we go outside, I need to get some information from your mom first."

A series of moans and groans followed from Tommy and Trevor as Jonathan walked to Ruth's desk.

"I know that I promised the kids a day out, but something is bothering me about this whole mess. Call it a hunch."

Puzzled, Ruth looked up at her brother and asked, "Like what?"

"I think the cause of the trouble goes back several years and the answer may actually lie in your library. What do you have about local history?"

Rising from her chair, Ruth said, "Come with me. I'll show you what I have." She led him to a section marked *Door County History*. With a wave of a hand she said, "You can begin here. A lot of tourists ask that question, so we put in a special section for them."

Jonathan grabbed several books from the shelves and retreated to a nearby chair. He opened each one, scanned the index page, and placed his selections into three stacks. After taking the last group of books back, he refreshed his search supply and returned to his chair. Repeating this process three times, only two groups of books remained. Starting with the books to his right, he went from index to content, making a few notes onto the sheet of paper he borrowed from his sister. He methodically moved to the next. When he was done, both sides of the sheet of paper were full of notes and his stomach growled.

He approached Tommy and Trevor. "How about a little ride after we get something to eat?" To which both of them gladly agreed.

"Sis, Could I borrow your car for a little while?"

"Sure—where you going?"

"The Sturgeon Bay Library. I may have stumbled upon something, but it requires further investigation. Stay here. I don't want you getting a lift home, even with the police presence. I'll be back before you're done working."

"Bye," the twins echoed, flanking their uncle as they left the building.

***

Trevor asked, "Can we play outside?" Prior to the events of the past few days, his question would not have required any serious thought. Ruth pushed her chair away from the table and rose, appearing to consider the request.

She cleared away some of the dinner dishes, and spoke with great exactness. "Right now, because of the danger, you or Tommy must never be left alone. For the present, either Uncle Jonathan, or I, will have to be with you both at all times."

"Cheer up," Jonathan chimed, trying to dispel the disappointment. "We'll go fishing in Kangaroo Lake tomorrow. That was on my to-do list." The prospect of a fishing outing turned their frowns into broad smiles. Having succeeded in brightening their mood, he said, "Now you two get into the living room, so your mom and I can finish cleaning up." Not having to be asked twice, the boys scampered out of the kitchen.

"You know, you're spoiling them."

"I know, but how often can I do this, Sis?" He said, while removing a couple of dishes from the table. "Besides, I want to tell you what I discovered at the Sturgeon Bay Library."

Amid the rattle of dishes, Jonathan began. "When I went to the library I wanted to follow some leads I culled from your collection of books. Once I'd gotten those facts, I started to peel back the layers of forgotten Door County history. What I was in search of was a murder that may have some connection to our current situation."

"How can a murder in the past have anything to do with the present?" Ruth asked, doubtingly.

"Rationally? Probably nothing, but as an archaeologist, and the theft of the Wabele, everything. Remember, the police are looking at this case from a practical perspective of criminal investigation. I think there may be more of a supernatural element to it."

Ruth appeared skeptical. "I know we all enjoy a good mystery or ghost story, but the reality of people being killed in my backyard eliminated any notion of a spiritual involvement from my perspective."

Sensing her apprehension, he softly related his theory. "I think the residue of evil lingers on long after the fact—like a poltergeist. Anyway, I looked for a murder that occurred somewhere around here.

"Door County isn't free of crime, and murder is a rare occurrence. Focused on that fact, my research produced three cases. One was a murder-suicide, the other involved a saloon brawl, but one concerned a revenge-robbery killing."

Ruth halted mid-washing of the dishes and stared with interest at her brother, whose last item generated a eureka moment in his tone.

"Yep—that one struck me, too, as a possible lead to pursue," he said with satisfaction. "That proved worthwhile and it resulted in an amazing tale."

Allowing the dishes to air-dry, Ruth took a seat at the kitchen table. Jonathan followed and sat across from her. He rested his arms on the table and leaned forward. "I found everything about this case in the Door County Advocate newspaper. It was on September 19 of 1892, that Joseph Warner went missing. A search party discovered his body, face down, head beaten into a mass of jelly, partially submerged in the water. The murder weapon, a club, was found nearby. It was the first murder in Door County where robbery was the motive.

"A ne'er-do-well, David Alperton, was seen by the lighthouse keeper by the point about the time of the murder. That, and a combination of Alperton having a considerable sum of money in his position and a large stain on his coat that looked like blood, justified his arrest. He tried to claim the money was recently given to him by his mother, but further investigation found that she had passed away six years prior. He also claimed that the *blood* on his coat was nothing more than tobacco that got wet.

"Warner, the murdered man, came here from Austria, worked hard, built a home and saved enough money to send for his wife. Not knowing of his death, she was grief-stricken when she arrived. The community was outraged by the crime and wanted justice.

"Alperton remained unsympathetic and denied any involvement in the beginning of the investigation, but after repeated questioning over a six-day period, he confessed. He was tried for murder and sentenced to life imprisonment in the Wisconsin State Prison in Waupun. As he was being led out of the court, he was reported to say that he would get his revenge on everyone, if it were the last thing he ever did. His outburst, upon conviction, was nothing new from criminals who had little to lose at that point."

"Wow! That's quite a story. Now I have to worry about ghosts, too?" Ruth mocked rhetorically

"Tomorrow, before going fishing, I want to tell Sheriff Collins what I found. It's only a hunch, but perhaps he could use his resources to find out what became of David Alperton. But for now, let's join the boys and watch some TV." Jonathan rose from the table and Ruth followed him into the living room's blue-glow.

***

"Good morning, sheriff," Jonathan said as he entered the front office.

"Good morning," Collins replied curtly. "Why don't you boys have a seat over there." He motioned toward a couple of chairs positioned in the corner, near the front window. Getting up from his chair he said, "Jonathan, please come with me into my office." Jonathan followed and Sheriff Collins quickly closed the door behind them.

"What's up?" Jonathan asked.

"It's been a hell-of-a-morning—the coroner's inquest, the body of Jacob being shipped back home and helping arrange Deputy William's funeral. His funeral, by the way, will be this Thursday. Sorry for my abruptness, but I guess I'm on overload, besides my lack of sleep." The sheriff looked haggard, with sagging bags under his eyes and a slept-in crinkled uniform. "What can I do for you today, Jonathan?" his polished veneer gone.

Hearing the sheriff's list of concerns, Jonathan reluctantly began. "What I am about to tell you may appear farfetched, but I think it may be important to what is going on."

After revealing the newspaper's account of David Alperton he added his own theory. "Perhaps, his spirit has retuned and he is taking revenge. I'm a scientist, and I know how ridiculous this all may sound, but there appears to be a parallel of players in this show. First the lighthouse keeper's daughter dies. It doesn't matter that the Coast Guard was not responsible for maintaining the lighthouse during Alperton's time, but cared for by the United States Lighthouse Establishment until 1910. His revenge is not necessarily on the Coast Guard, but on the occupation of lighthouse keeper. Next follows Jacob, who may have known something and was in the wrong place at the wrong time. Lastly your deputy—a surrogate symbol of the justice system that was responsible for his arrest and imprisonment."

Sitting silent for some time, Sheriff Collins finally spoke. "Okay. What the hell. I'll send an inquiry to the state pen and see what happened to Mister Alperton. At this point, I am ready to believe in almost anything.

Now if you will excuse me, I've got a lot on my plate."

Taking the cue to leave, Jonathan gathered the twins and went outside. Although the trip was later in the day than he wanted, because the best fishing was early in the morning, their next stops were the bait shop and Kangaroo Lake.

**

Jonathan parked his sister's car midway along the narrow shoulder on the north embankment of the causeway. A warm steady southern breeze bathed the road, helping to curb the noonday heat. As they crossed to the south side of the road, the wind and sun made them squint as they scanned the water's edge for a suitable fishing spot. Not surprisingly, Tommy and Trevor selected the same spot.

"Hey! Uncle Jonathan! Tommy's fishing in my spot," Trevor protested.

"I brought you two out here to fish, not fight." Jonathan's response was more conciliatory than reprimand. "Tommy, you sit there," pointing to a section of large rocks that extended a bit into the lake. "And Trevor, you can sit on my left side along this bank."

No sooner were their hooks baited and in the water when Tommy yelled, "I got a bite!" The red and white bobber plunged into the glare of the sun's sparkling reflection on the lake. The calm erupted into a splattering of water, sending fleeing ripples pulsing from the taut fishing line. Tommy pulled on his bamboo pole, making it arc from the strain. Stepping backward toward the road, he slipped on the moss-laden rocks that lined the causeway, falling on his rear end. Trevor laughed and went to assist his mortified brother.

"Good catch, Tommy," praised Jonathan, as a large perch was pulled from the water. The fish began to flop about on the road's tarmac. Tommy tried to hold it in place but with little success until his uncle came to the rescue.

"I'll get the bucket from the car," Tommy volunteered, and ran across the road. As he returned with the metal bucket the advancing roar of a car's engine caught the attention of Jonathan. Approaching from the east end of the roadway the vehicle appeared to accelerate and bear down on Tommy.

"Tommy! The car!" Jonathan shouted.

Instinctively, hearing the oncoming noise, Tommy glanced over his left shoulder and froze. Observing his delay, Jonathan sprinted diagonally across the road, grabbed him by the waist and the two of them rolled onto the pavement and down the opposite embankment. The pair's fall ended as they splashed into the brackish waters of the swampy side of the causeway.

Missing them by inches, the gray 1950 Packard ambulance abruptly swerved to the left toward Trevor, who was paralyzed by the unexpected chain of events. Standing safely below grade of the highway, on the graveled shoulder, the hot exhaust of the fleeing car washed over his body as it fled west. In that brief second he was able to recognize the driver as Mister Devlin.

***

"What happened to you two?" Sheriff Collins asked, astonished at the scruffy appearance of Jonathan and Tommy.

"We were nearly killed while fishing off the causeway on County Road E. It wasn't by accident either," Jonathan said, still shaken by the experience. "Trevor was able to see who was at the wheel and that person was none other than Mister Devlin. He tried to intentionally run-down Tommy, but I was able to push him out of the way. "This," pointing to Tommy's tattered clothing, "is the result."

"Any serious injuries?" the sheriff asked, as he rose from the desk and toward the trio.

"I don't think so—some bruises and a few minor cuts. I took the brunt from the tumble. I wanted to stop here first and let you know what happened before telling Ruth."

"You bet. Why don't you and Tommy go get yourselves cleaned up in the bathroom. I'll take your statement and make out an official report when you get out."

After a quick cleanup, Trevor, Tommy, and their uncle Jonathan took seats opposite the sheriff at his desk. "I don't think there is any doubt that Mister Devlin is our chief suspect, but his true identity remains a mystery," Sheriff Collins reflected. "In fact, that scarf found at the murder scene of Deputy Richard Williams, turned out to be the type used in the theatrical trades—the likes of magicians and clowns. But, it's not as if this guy has any address that we can follow up with a visit."

Jonathan nodded and asked," Did you hear from the state prison about David Alperton?"

"Nope, not yet, but I expect to hear something by this evening. For now, keep out of sight as much as you can. I will continue the extra surveillance at your sister's house, but our resources are thin already. You better go now and tell Ruth. If you have any other ideas, any, I want to hear them." The sheriff ushered everyone to the door and held it open while they filed past.

***

"Don't tell me that you boys got a big fish that pulled you into the water?" Ruth teased after seeing her brother's scruffy appearance.

"Not quite, but we did have an adventure," he replied somberly.

Sensing something more serious, she asked warily, "What happened?"

"Tommy almost got killed and Uncle Jonathan saved him," Trevor blurted.

"What!" Ruth cried in disbelief. Moving from behind her desk she approached Tommy and frantically checked him over.

"We're all a little shaken up. Boys, why don't you two go over there," Jonathan pointed to the far end of the library. "It's okay now. I'll tell you everything. Can we talk in private?" he asked Ruth, observing a few of the library's patrons glance in their direction at Trevor's outburst.

"Sure. Helen, I'll be in the back room for a while. Will you please handle the desk?" Ruth asked as she led her brother into her private office.

Jonathan's account of the incident was less detailed in its closeness of being nearly killed, out of concern for Ruth's heightened unease. He did not, however, minimize the need to be on alert. "No one should ever be left alone until this clown, or whatever he is, is finally caught. Perhaps Tommy is most at risk, because his actions with the Wabele helmet triggered something beyond our understanding."

"What do we do now?" Ruth asked, with a hesitant tone.

"If we look at all the facts, I would say Mister Devlin is definitely connected to all this. I intend to find out how."

Her brother's words conjured up more mystery than resolution and in her current state of uncertainly she pressed the question. "Are we safe in our house, or for that matter, are we safe anywhere?" Her normal confident composure nearly exhausted as she searched her brother for reassurances.

"We are safe as we can be just being together," Jonathan said, trying to sooth his sister's fear. "Also, the fact that we have a two-man, twenty-four hour stakeout at your house probably makes that place even safer."

Forcing a smile, Ruth slowly nodded.

"Now, try not to worry. I'm going to leave Trevor with you so Tommy and I can go back to the house, shower; change clothes, put on some dry shoes, too. I smell of swamp."

"Yes, you do," Ruth agreed, displaying a smile, the first real one since the murders.

***

Jonathan and Tommy returned after only a short absence. Tommy, preceding his uncle into the library, did not appear happy. "It can't be helped, you'll have to stay inside for now," Jonathan said. "Go and keep your brother company." He motioned to where Trevor was sitting, equally grim-faced.

"What's up with Tommy?" Ruth asked.

"The usual. He doesn't seem to understand the seriousness of the situation. Even after that close call this morning." Jonathan stood next to Ruth's desk and asked, "May I use your phone to call the museum? I can make it collect. Also, I could use a steno pad."

"Sure, no problem and you don't have to make it collect either." Handing him a spiral notebook she gestured toward her office at the rear of the library. "You'll probably want some privacy too, so use the phone in my office."

Nearly a half-hour elapsed before Jonathan emerged from Ruth's office. He held the notebook high in the air and waved to his sister. "I know you're about to close, so I'll be quick," he said and walked toward the 500 numbered bookcase. He reappeared after only ten minutes and asked, "Do you have the current edition of *Sky and Telescope?*"

Ruth nodded and motioned toward the periodical section. "Your mood has changed since you made your phone call. What's up?"

"I need to check on a date. If my suspicions are correct, I think I may have solved the why and wherefore of this mystery." Finding the magazine, he jotted something in his notebook, turned toward Ruth and exclaimed, "I'm done! Let's go."

"Are you going to share your information?" Ruth asked, visibly irritated by Jonathan's secretiveness.

"You bet, Sis. How about over dinner at Bailey's?"

"Based on what you said, and what happened when you went fishing, are you sure it's safe to go out?" Ruth probed her brother for reassurance.

"Look, Sis, we have to eat and Bailey's is a very public place," Jonathan argued. "We can't live in fear."

"When you put it that way, I suppose you're right. How can I refuse?" she said, half-heartedly agreeing to the offer. "C'mon boys, your uncle wants to spend all of his money on the way to the poorhouse." Her mocking tone tried to conceal her distress and fear for their safety.

"Yeah!" Trevor exclaimed and began to charge out of the building with Tommy close behind.

Ruth yelled, "Stop!"

Her sternness in the command made the boys freeze in place until she reached them. "You will stay close to us at all times," she admonished. "Do you understand?"

"Uh-hu," they apologetically agreed.

***

"Bailey's is a bit crowded for a Tuesday," Jonathan remarked.

Ruth casually commented. "You can thank the tourist season for that. I guess you would fall into that category, too."

"It's good that we came right after the library closed. I think if we were any later we would have to wait," Jonathan said, as they were escorted to a table.

Having placed their order, Jonathan gave Tommy and Trevor some money to play the pinball machine. Ruth prodded her brother, "Okay, now it's your turn. What did you learn from your call to the museum?"

"I talked with my associate, Professor McGookgan; she is an anthropologist with the museum and has a better understanding of the social patterns and ritual practices of the Poro Society. She told me the Wabele mask, sometimes referred to as a Wanyugo mask, benefits their society, by acknowledging evil, and at the same time combating it. The wearer, usually a high priest, has the ability to conjure up the dead. I think Tommy unwittingly did just that and it came in the form of a clown. Why a clown? I don't know, maybe it's some perverse idea of a joke."

"Did you discuss this with Sheriff Collins?"

"Somewhat, but I only told him of my suspicions involving a physical association with the mask and the murderer David Alperton. I was alluding to the possibility of someone using a local legend to mask, no pun intended, something more nefarious. I now think, based upon what Professor McGookgan told me, we may have a case of spiritual possession by an evil entity." Jonathan sat back in his chair and let his verdict sink in.

"Unbelievable," Ruth uttered "How did you get the mask in the first place—I mean, knowing some of the dangers surrounding it?"

"As you know, I have been adding to my private collection of artifacts for years. I purchased the Wabele mask from a shaman, who, as I can recall, appeared rather eager to sell it. I really didn't see a problem at the time because I wasn't going to wear it. I didn't even believe in its magical capabilities." Jonathan hesitated and looked at his sister for forgiveness. "Knowing the inquisitive nature of kids, I should have been more careful."

"Don't blame yourself." Ruth tried to dismiss her brother's confession and feelings of guilt. "Those boys shouldn't have been snooping around your things anyway."

Jonathan responded with a half-smile, and continued. "It turns out the mask by itself wouldn't trigger any result, but the wearer needs to cover himself with a costume made from cotton to be effective. I say 'himself' because it only pertains to males. When Tommy placed that sheet over his body he put on a costume—a ghost's costume! The Poro Society has a great fear of the power of the mask. And for that very reason keep it hidden in an isolated place far from the village, in a sacred grove. Because Tommy can see Mister Devlin for the criminal he really is, it makes Tommy a target."

Ruth drew a breath. "What can we do? How do we fight this—this thing?"

"Whatever it is, it has form. That is also consistent with Poro folklore about bringing the dead back to life. It obviously can kill and drive a car, so physically it probably has some human vulnerability until it converts itself into pure evil. What's unusual about this is the fact that Mister Devlin is in control of the mask—and there will be a full-moon on the first of July."

"What does that have to do with everything you told me so far?"

"Oh, I'm sorry; I unintentionally skipped the linchpin concerning a rite of the Poro Society." Jonathan studied his sister's reaction "Like all primitive societies, the moon has an important role in many rituals.

"The full-moon is a time that produces amplification of power. It becomes a time of renewal, a time to cast off things that no longer serve you. When Mister Devlin dons the Wabele mask, on the night of a full moon, he will become one with it and assume all the magical powers of the mask. You see, Tommy's actions made him recognize evil and conjure up a restless spirit in the form of Mister Devlin. But, if that evil unites with the ability of the mask, the resulting merger will bring about bad juju."

"Bad juju? What's bad juju?"

Before he could answer her, the waitress returned with their order. "Here you are four orders of spaghetti with meatballs," the waitress said with an effervescent lilt in her voice.

Ruth began to get up from the table and retrieve her boys when Jonathan said, "Sit, Sis. I'll get them."

The prospect of eating overruled playing with the pinball machine and they eagerly followed their uncle back to the table. After saying grace, Ruth shot a probing look at her brother and indirectly pushed him for a response, "Don't leave me hanging."

"It's a spell and no one knows the consequences, because it has never been done. The effects are unknown, but I'm certain it won't be good."

"What's unknown?" Trevor asked.

"Nothing you have to be concerned about, young man," Ruth replied. "Just eat your meal."

***

When they returned home, Ruth suggested they play Monopoly, a favorite of the boys. After setting up the game and distributing small stacks of play-money, the noise of an approaching vehicle caught their attention. It was followed by a knock on the door.

Looking through the window, Jonathan saw Sheriff Collins. "What brings you here tonight, sheriff?" Jonathan asked as he opened the door to let him in.

He noticed the game on the kitchen table and said, "I won't be too long. I got a call from the warden at Waupun about that fella, David Alperton. I thought you would want hear what he said."

"Boys," Ruth said, "go and get into your p.j.'s."

With only Jonathan and Ruth remaining, the sheriff began, "Turns out that our Mister Alperton was quite a character. He was convicted of first-degree murder and sentenced to life imprisonment. That was in 1892. His record shows that he was quite a troublemaker, serving several months in solitary confinement. In September of 1898 Alperton was transferred from Waupun to the newly constructed Wisconsin State Reformatory in Green Bay. It was there, on June 9, 1899, that another prisoner probably killed David Alperton. I say probably, because his murderer was never identified."

"How did he die?" asked Jonathan.

"He was strangled with a sheet, while working in the prison laundry. All the other prisoners claim they didn't see anything," Sheriff Collins said sarcastically. "It was made to look like an accident with the sheet twisted around his neck. The other end was wrapped around an exposed pulley from one of the laundry machines."

"Did he have any relatives that could possibly carry on a generation-to-generation vendetta against the current residents of our area?" Ruth asked.

"No. It appears that Alperton was the last in his family's line. His mother died six years prior to his arrest. Speculating that his ghost is responsible for these crimes is a bit farfetched. If I were to issue an all-points bulletin about a ghost, I'd be laughed out of Door County. Right now, having to describe the suspect as a clown makes me a bit uncomfortable and I'm afraid the announcement alone will carry some skepticism and ridicule. Richard's funeral is a couple of days away, and I'm in no mood for foolishness." The sheriff finished and caught himself staring into space, then glanced at the Monopoly board again. "Oh, I've taken enough of your time. I've got to get some sleep." He moved toward the outside door. Stopping in front of the door, he turned, and added, "By the way, I did notify the Wisconsin State Patrol about the gray 1950

Packard ambulance. So far, nothing. But something as unusual as that doesn't disappear into thin air. Well, I gotta run, goodnight," he said, as he opened the door and hurried out.

"Poor guy, I feel sorry for him," Ruth said.

"Yeah, me, too," Jonathan agreed.

"Why didn't you tell Sheriff Collins about what you discovered about the Poro Society and their rituals?"

"I hinted at my suspicions when I filed the report after the fishing incident. He doesn't seem too keen on any spiritual connection, so I didn't want to push it. After all, he's the investigator and I'm the archeologist," Jonathan said, as the twins filed back into the kitchen.

The combination of full stomachs and exhaustion from the day's events resulted in a mutual postponement of the game with less than an hour of play. After everyone retired, the house became still with the only activity coming from the roving patrol outside.

A waxing gibbous moon hung low on the horizon. Trees cast long spectral barbs that knitted a shadowy blanket over the dew-laden ground. A few minutes past midnight, darkness consumed the land as the moon descended beyond the horizon—even the howling of faraway coyotes was engulfed in the blackness.

A shade within a shadow, Mister Devlin slithered though the night. Avoiding the dimly lit porch light of the house, he edged his way to Trevor's bedroom window. He then twisted the four window screen turn buttons to a vertical position and quietly removed the screen and frame assembly from the window; the inner hooks carelessly left unattached. Standing in full frame of the windowpane he lightly tapped on the glass, attempting to get Trevor's attention.

Awakened by the sound, Trevor tried to focus on the form outside his window. Soon the figure transformed itself into someone that he knew—it was his father. His father died when he was two years old, but he recognized him from the picture that hung on the living room wall. "Dad?" he whispered.

Beyond, the shape nodded and motioned Trevor to unlatch the window. He placed his index finger over his lips as a sign for silence. Trevor obliged the request, and slowly pulled open the sash.

Reaching over the windowsill his *father* took hold of Trevor's trusting hands and helped him into the night.

***

"Where's Trevor?" asked Tommy, as he entered the kitchen.

"He's probably in the bathroom." Ruth said, hurriedly preparing the French toast batter.

"No, he's not. I was just there."

Jonathan sniffed the air as he entered the kitchen. "Ah, the smell of bacon, love it." Noticing his sister's look of concern, he asked, "What's up?"

"Tommy wanted to know where Trevor is."

"Don't worry, Sis, I'll have a look. He's probably playing some kind of game with us. I don't think he realizes how serious the situation is to joke about this stuff," Jonathan said gently, trying to ease his sister's worries. "C'mon, Tommy, let's find that little brat."

"Did you unlock that, Tommy?" his uncle asked, pointing to the partially opened window.

"No. It was that way when I got up."

Frantically Jonathan raced to the window and raised the sash. Sticking his head outside, he noticed the flattened grass, heavy laden with the morning's dew. The screen, positioned to his right, lay slanted against the house. "Trevor!" he yelled in panic. "Trevor! Trevor!" Again, bellowing into the morning air.

His cries alerted one of the officers on patrol who emerged from the far side of the house, puzzled by the disturbance. "Is everything okay?" he queried.

"No!" Jonathan shot back. "Trevor's missing and I don't know if he's been taken, or playing a game."

Ruth arrived at the doorway of the boys' bedroom, her eyes wide. "What's happening? Did the police patrol see him?" Her voice strained with emotion.

"Take it easy, Sis. I'll go outside and check around. I'm sure he's okay," Jonathan said, trying to remain calm.

"I'm going outside, too!" she shot back and in a tone that defied any notion of stopping her.

In her haste to see what happened to Trevor, the bacon that once had an enticing smell now smoked. Ruth turned off the flame under the frying pan and quickly pitched it into the sink, dousing it with water. It sizzled under the flow and a cloud of steam erupted into the air. She threw on a light jacket, then followed Tommy and her brother outside.

"It looks like he climbed out of his bedroom window. I think we should start our search from there," the officer suggested.

"Okay." Jonathan said, and hastily assembled the group, herding them to the side of the house.

"Careful, don't step on any tracks," the officer cautioned.

When they reached the spot below the window, the duty officer said," Stay here; I want to see where this trampled grass trail leads."

Ruth, restless, scanned the nearby woods looking for any sign of her boy. She pleaded, "Can't we do something? I don't want to wait around here.

"We can't go off on a wild goose chase without some plan!" Jonathan sharply countered.

"If this maniac can kill a young man and a deputy, don't you think Trevor's in grave danger, too?" Ruth bawled.

Jonathan held Ruth as she started to sob. He tried to calm her, gently stroking her back.

The officer returned with a troubled look on his face. "I followed the trail until it ended at the main road. There were no tire impressions on this side of the highway, so I crossed over to the opposite embankment. I did find evidence of a vehicle having parked there. It was farther in the heavy brush, but not so far in as to escape notice during our rounds. I don't know how we could have missed it. I have to radio this in."

When Sheriff Collins arrived, both Ruth and Jonathan charged outside to meet him. Before either of them could speak, the sheriff said, "I have ordered roadblocks south of here, on the two main highways, and begun organizing search parties looking for Trevor."

"What can we do?" Ruth anxiously asked.

"For one, I will need a copy of the most recent picture of Trevor. Our office will be the command center as we plan the search area. You are welcome to assist our staff, Ruth."

"I'll get the picture, but I want to look for my son now!" Ruth demanded. "You don't understand, Bob. My son is out there with a killer and you expect me to sit tight!" Her words bolted from her mouth with rage and frustration.

"Ruth, I understand, but what are you going to do that we aren't doing now?" Sheriff Collins asked firmly. "Please, get the photograph."

"You're right, Bob, but I'm his mother," she grudgingly agreed and left.

"Sheriff," Jonathan spoke up, "I want to help in the search, too."

"By all means—Jonathan. Stop by the office...pick up a grid map. We use them to prevent any duplication of the search areas." Sheriff Collins said, clearly troubled after his exchange with Ruth.

Ruth returned with Trevor's last school portrait and handed it to the sheriff.

Taking the picture, Sheriff Collins again offered Ruth an opportunity for her involvement. "I could really use your help at the office. With you there I can free up one of my deputies."

"I would like that. At least I won't feel so helpless," she said and forced a pained smile. "I have to phone the library first and tell Helen what's happing. I'll be over—after that, Bob." Ruth, clearly agitated, appeared ready to pounce on anyone who would hinder her resolve.

Returning a sympathetic smile, the sheriff said," I know this is tough, but we will find Trevor. I promise."

"I have to believe that Bob, or else I will...," she sobbed, never finishing her thought. Wells of tears formed in her eyes as she abruptly turned toward the house.

Ruth regained her composure by the time she entered the kitchen, and then called out, "Jonathan and Tommy come here."

Her call was immediately answered by the appearance of her brother and son. "What's up?" Jonathan asked.

"You need to eat," Ruth said in an ordering tone. "Sorry about the bacon, but the French toast will have to do. We can't send you out without some fuel." Ruth moved robotically toward the stove.

***

When Jonathan returned home with Tommy he found Ruth sitting on the couch across from Sheriff Collins, who rested on a brown leather easy chair. "After my shift, Bob brought me home," Ruth said. "I thought it would be nice to have some company and I also invited him to stay for dinner. It won't be much—brats and buns. I really don't feel like eating," she said lethargically. "Jonathan, will you please start the charcoal grill? Tommy will show where everything is."

"Sure thing, Sis."

***

The dinner conversation was guarded, knowing Ruth's fragile state. Sheriff Collins offered some plans involving the search, trying to reinforce the magnitude of the efforts that were underway for her peace of mind. Tommy remained quiet throughout the meal and Ruth picked languidly at her food, never really eating.

The conversation turned to tomorrow's funeral for the slain deputy. "Due to the ongoing search, my appearance will be brief," Sheriff Collins apologized.

Jonathan nodded. "I think everyone understands the situation and the need to continue the investigation and hunt."

"I really haven't come to terms with the death of Richard," Sheriff Collins unexpectedly revealed his own emotional pain.

An uneasy silence followed.

Breaking the awkward stillness, Jonathan asked, "Bob, did you consider the possibility of our Mister Devlin using a boat to get away?"

"That did occur to me, too, so I informed the Coast Guard to be on the lookout," ending his own reflection on the loss of his deputy. "Total involvement by them is officially beyond their jurisdiction. Although, when I talked with Chief Barnes about your theories, and Devlin's possible involvement with the death of his daughter, he was eager to do anything within his power to assist."

"Well, I think I'll get moving. I have to stop by the office, get my dress uniform ready for tomorrow, and review my part of the eulogy. Thanks again."

"No. Thank you, Bob. I'm a bundle of nervous energy and need to stay active, or else lose my mind. I needed this as much as you," she said warmly, while rising.

The sheriff rose from his chair and extended a parting handshake toward Ruth. Taking the back of his hand, she pulled it toward herself, allowing it to touch her waist. Her other hand reached around his back and gave him a tender hug, which he returned in kind. At that moment Ruth's self-restraint could not hold back the emotion that was welled up inside and she began to weep bitterly, her body trembling against his.

"Come on, Tommy, let's get ready for bed," Jonathan urged, saddened by his sister's display of grief.

Saying nothing, Sheriff Collins remained still and allowed Ruth her emotional release. Recovering, she moved backward and grabbed a napkin from the kitchen table.

"I'm sorry Bob, I am sick with worry about Trevor," Ruth said while blotting away the tears from her eyes with the napkin.

"You don't have to apologize to me. I understand."

Bidding him a good night she locked the door and went in search of her brother. She found him in the living room, lying on the couch and staring up at the ceiling. "Jonathan, I'm beat and you're probably, too. I won't be functional tomorrow if I don't get some rest."

"Don't worry about me, Sis. I'll take care of cleaning up the kitchen. You just try to get some sleep."

"Also, would you mind sleeping in Trevor's bed tonight? I would feel more comfortable knowing you were in the same room with Tommy."

"I don't mind, as long as Tommy doesn't object to my snoring," he joked, trying to lessen the tension.

The attempt at humor fell flat. Ruth, preoccupied with worry replied lethargy. "Tommy won't mind. In fact, he's the one that asked me to ask you. He's scared of sleeping alone and would be relieved to have an adult nearby while he slept."

***

With great emotional anxiety they got an early start the next day. Unrested, few words were spoken as each one silently contemplated what the day had in store. Ruth, feeling a burn in her stomach, forced down a piece of dry toast. Taking care of themselves, Jonathan and Tommy fixed bowls of cereal, which neither of them completely finished. Likewise, the ride into town was silent except for the sound of the car's engine. It wasn't until they reached the sheriff's office that Ruth expressed her wishes.

As Ruth, Jonathan, and Tommy entered the sheriff's office, she quietly instructed Jonathan, "Pick me up at ten o'clock. I want all of us to attend the service together. I need both of you by my side. I know that I can't do this by myself. You understand, don't you?"

"Sure thing, Sis," Jonathan softly agreed. Once inside, he spotted the sheriff, looking weary, attired in his dress uniform. He was mulling over a large wall map of Door County speckled with various colored pins. Offering a subdued morning greeting, he asked somberly, "What area do you want me to explore today, sheriff?"

He acknowledged Jonathan's greeting with an equal amount of restraint and said, "Why don't you ride out on Highway Q, take Stone Mill Road and check those seasonal cottages along Moonlight Bay. It shouldn't be too difficult. If the cabins are occupied—ask the people if they have noticed anything unusual. If the buildings are unoccupied—make sure that they haven't been broken into."

"Bob," Jonathan said, in a more familiar tone. "I'm not in uniform and my presence may appear suspicious."

"You're right," he agreed and opened the top drawer of the desk. Sheriff Collins pulled out a badge and handed it to Jonathan. "I hereby deputize you until we find our culprit and Trevor. Also, take some of these fliers and hand them out when you make your rounds. If you see anything strange, don't try to be a hero. Get back here or call me and I'll handle it. Lastly, make sure you keep that badge visible at all times."

***

Jonathan made his way north along highway Q and carefully scanned the edges of the road. Tommy, pretending to be his uncle's co-pilot, sat on the passenger side of the car. They looked for any telltale evidence of a vehicle's abnormal exit off the road and entry into the dense forest.

Having reached the Stone Mill Road intersection, Jonathan followed its curved path south. He stopped at several of the vacation cottages and cabins, but found only three that were occupied. Being seasonal vacationers, all of those inhabitants appeared unaware of Trevor's kidnapping. The remaining vacant properties did not look as if they had been disturbed in any way. The assignment completed, he retraced his path back to town.

The death of Deputy Richard Williams generated overwhelming public sympathy. Support also came from all of the police departments in Door County, the Wisconsin State Patrol, and some adjoining districts. Interspersed among the mourners were the individual blue, gray and brown uniforms of those law enforcement units. All came to honor his memory, give emotional support to his wife and two children, but deep inside wanted retribution for the crime.

At the conclusion of the requiem Mass, the casket of Deputy Williams passed through a phalanx of police officers who rendered a hand salute in tribute to their fallen comrade. His widow, clothed in a black dress, followed behind and with difficult steps, moved in a trancelike state, her two children clinging to her. As the procession of cars traveled west to Saint Mary of the Lake Cemetery, a curtain of clouds moved inland off Lake Michigan and cloaked the motorcade. Casting a shadow over the town, it was as if the sun itself grieved for the loss by hiding its rays.

***

With nearly the entire community involved in a collective mourning, Mister Devlin covertly stole his way into town while the funeral service took place. Traveling west on Bluff Road, he turned north and meandered along a rustic ridge road. Finding some dense cover in the woods, he got out of his gray ambulance and trekked over the ridge, which overlooked the cemetery. He was alone.

Picking a choice spot he sat and waited. He bore no remorse as the cars accumulated below. In fact, he was overjoyed at the misery he caused. Under his attentive gaze he saw people leaving their cars, *like ants* he thought, *gathering around a hole in the ground*. Smiling at the scene, he regretted that he was too far away to hear their sobs. He wanted to see the tears of the mourners. *Yes, wouldn't that be amusing to catch the snivels of the multitude close at hand.*

Having achieved his goal of savoring the misery, even at a distance, he departed, gratified at the loss the community felt. He was happy in the thought of inflicting sorrow on the town that he despised so much.

***

As soon as Jonathan and Tommy had something to eat at the funeral brunch, they were on the road again. Filled with reflective silence, neither spoke.

Tommy stared blankly at the passing trees and lamented. "I'm sorry Uncle Jonathan."

Taking his eyes off the road for a few seconds he eyed his nephew. "Sorry?"

After a slight pause, Tommy spoke uneasily. "If I didn't put on that mask none of this would have happened. That policeman, Jacob and maybe even Angelica would still be alive."

Jonathan slowly turned onto the shoulder of the road and put the car in park. Carefully searching for the words, he offered some consolatory insight. "Tommy, there is evil in the world and you are not responsible for its existence. If anyone is to blame, it is me for even bringing the mask into your house." Gently messing Tommy's sandy colored hair with his right hand, he added, "Don't worry, we'll find Trevor. I promise."

He placed the idling car back in gear and resumed his drive, their destination the Point Lighthouse and the surrounding cottages. The overcast sky began to thicken. Soon droplets of rain formed on the dust-covered window. Jonathan turned on the wipers and an opaque film streaked across the curved glass. His eyes strained to look beyond the dirt-veiled view. After a short while, the pounding rain cleared the windshield, the thrashing blades fighting to keep up with the sudden downpour.

By the time they arrived at the lighthouse the wind and rain made any attempt at searching for Trevor almost impossible. The fog concealed the structure from view, presenting the illusion of a light mysteriously suspended in the murkiness. Traveling towards The Point, the car's headlights barely broke through the wall of falling water in front of them. The road became a small river, connecting miniature lakes, obscuring the uneven surfaces they traveled over. They bounced and sloshed their way until reaching the end of the road. Jonathan carefully turned the vehicle around, careful not to go beyond the limits of the gravel road and sink into the muddy shoulder.

"It looks like we will have to do this again tomorrow, Tommy," Jonathan said, as he slowly maneuvered his way back to town.

Tommy remained silent.

When they reached the main highway travel became less bumpy but the occasional encounter with oncoming traffic made Jonathan squint into the approaching headlights. As each vehicle passed, a splash of water descended over the car's windshield, further concealing the road, making travel more treacherous. By the time they reached town the rain had letup slightly.

When Jonathan approached the police station, he sounded the car's horn, announcing his arrival. His sister, standing inside behind the front window, acknowledged the signal with a wave. As she ran through the rain to the waiting car, Tommy hopped over the seat to the back, letting his mother have the front passenger's side of the car.

No sooner was Ruth inside then she immediately broke the news. "One of the tourists thought they saw a gray ambulance around town at the time of the funeral." Breathless, she wiped her wet face with her bare hand.

"Did that person notice in which direction it was traveling?"

"Yes. At the time it was traveling east, in the direction of the lake. When we got the news, Sheriff Collins personally went out, but between the time of the report and action, it was old news."

"But, that has to be good news, knowing that he is still in the area. Don't you think?"

"Of course, that was the first good news I heard. The sheriff was also encouraged by it. In fact, everyone in the office was cheered up by the announcement. Following the sadness of the funeral, it brought a glimmer of hope."

"Did anyone get a look at the driver, or see if there was a passenger?" Jonathan asked cautiously, afraid his question might invoke more pain on his sister, who was already tormented with enough anguish.

Ruth did not respond immediately. Instead, she stared out the front window and seemingly beyond the rain-filled day. "No," she finally said. After another contemplative pause, she spoke. "Would you mind making something for dinner tonight for you and Tommy? I'm worn out and not really very hungry. I think I'll go to bed when we get home."

"Okay, Sis, but you have to keep up your strength, too."

"I know. I did have something at the funeral brunch. I need rest more than food right now, I don't have the appetite. I'll eat something in the morning."

Jonathan knew that she would have another restless night. Like the previous night, he would hear his sister pacing the floors as he, too, struggled, and not knowing of Trevor's fate.

***

"According to the WDOR weather report, it sounds like we're going to have light showers today, with a chance of an isolated storm," Sheriff Collins told the gathering in his office. "I'll be going out to the Sister Bay area, the Wisconsin State Patrol contingent will be checking out Northport and adjoining parks, and the Ephraim police department will expand their own search area."

Jonathan raised his hand and asked, "Where do you want me to look today, Sheriff?"

"I know it was raining pretty hard yesterday afternoon, so you probably can finish up the area around The Point Light. When you come back, why don't you swing around Ridge Road and check that area along the harbor range lights." Sheriff Collins turned around and faced the wall map of the county. Touching the map, he made a sweeping motion over the northeast end of the harbor. Commenting on the area, he said, "Not too many places out that way, so it shouldn't take long."

"Jonathan, are you certain Tommy is safe being with you?" Ruth asked, with an apprehensive tone.

"Don't worry, Sis. First of all, I don't think Tommy wants to sit in this office for eight or ten hours, because you really can't allow him out of your sight. And besides, Tommy gives me an extra set of eyes. Right, Tommy?" Jonathan said, giving him a wink.

"Speaking of an extra set of eyes, would you like to accompany me, Ruth, when I go out to the bay area?" Sheriff Collins asked. "I think Gary Simons can handle the office for today and it will be good for you to get out."

Ruth's demeanor brightened. "I like that idea a lot, Bob. I was going to ask if I could go out on one of the patrols."

Jonathan made his way toward the door. "Well, Tommy and I better get going. The rain will slow us down a bit, but I don't think it will be as bad as yesterday afternoon."

***

After visiting several of the vacation homes around The Point Light, they traveled down a few dead-end roads that terminated at the lake. Jonathan appeared more relaxed as he made his opening speech each time he introduced himself as a deputy sheriff. Many of the cottages were occupied with disappointed vacationers forced inside because of the rain—helpful because it assisted in spreading the news of the kidnapping.

Shortly after one o'clock, Jonathan headed out along the Old Point Road and decided that it was time to take a break. Besides the continuous drizzle, the temperature stayed on the cool side, forcing them to remain in the car as they ate their lunch. In an effort to save time, by not having to go into town to eat, Jonathan had made a couple of ham and cheese sandwiches at home that morning. For a beverage, he packed two bottles of Orange Crush soda.

"How are you doing?" he asked Tommy, studying him for any signs of distress.

Finishing the bite from his sandwich, Tommy forced a smile, "Okay, Uncle—but I really miss Trevor."

"So do I, Tommy." Jonathan's gaze wandered over and beyond the dashboard, surveying the unusual impressionistic looking landscape through the rain-speckled windshield. The mournful sound of a distant foghorn captured their own melancholy mood.

While eating their lunches, Jonathan paused and pulled out the two bottles of soda from the metal cooler on the back seat. "Oh, I forgot the bottle opener," he said with a disappointed tone.

"Don't worry, Uncle. I have my Cub Scout knife," Tommy said, and proudly pulled the knife from his pocket.

Accepting it with a smile, Jonathan used its opener to pop open the bottles. Finished with their sodas, Jonathan went outside to relieve himself in the brush. Tommy followed his uncle's lead, but moved a little farther up the trail. Done, Jonathan turned toward their car. Noticing a muted glint of metal intermixed within the wet foliage near the shore, he pushed his way through the brush. Finding its source, it proved to be a chrome spotlight attached to a gray, 1950 Packard ambulance.

Tommy, unaware of his uncle's discovery, returned to the car and went inside, out of the light rain. No sooner did he seat himself then the passenger door suddenly flung open, catching Tommy by surprise.

"I've found the ambulance!" Jonathan shouted, breathless and barely able to contain his excitement. "Come with me," he coaxed Tommy outside.

"Wow!" Tommy exclaimed, seeing the gray vehicle deliberately concealed in the thick undergrowth. "What do we do now, Uncle?"

"I'm not sure. Trevor could be right around here. If we go into town and tell the sheriff they could escape. First, let's follow this footpath toward the lake."

Breaking out of the tree line along the beach, the twisted footpath ended. A small weathered pier, having barely enough planking attached to its lateral beams, stood partially submerged at the water's edge. Beyond that and in front of them, across a lagoon with a narrow inlet, fed by the waters of the lake, a spit of land formed a barrier between them and the harbor. On the far left side of the finger of land, the silhouetted skeletal relic of 'Old Bailey's' light stood like a silent sentinel.

"Trevor is over there," Tommy said, pointing to the abandoned lighthouse.

"How do you know that, Tommy?"

"I can feel it. We have to save him! We need to go there now!"

"We will, but we can't rush over there without a plan. I would guess that Mister Devlin parked the ambulance here and took a boat across the lagoon." Deep in thought for several minutes, he finally spoke. "I agree...we have to act now. Let's get into the car."

Jonathan frantically turned the car around and sped down the deserted road. He reached the fork in the road and turned left. Continuing down another road he stopped short of the end, preferring the concealment of the forest between him and the lighthouse. Beyond the trees, the isthmus was covered with large rocks, a few stands of trees, and isolated sandbars, making continued travel somewhat difficult. Rainsqualls began to pummel them, replacing the light drizzle that shadowed them most of the day.

"Tommy, listen to me. I want you to stay in this car. When I go, lock all the doors and under no circumstance open them. If, by some chance, Mister Devlin comes here, use the car's horn to get someone's attention." Looking directly into Tommy's eyes, he forcefully asked, "Do you understand?"

Squirming in place and nervous, Tommy replied. "Yes. I understand."

Jonathan pulled up the collar of his jacket and put on his weathered hat, the one he habitually wore on his archeological digs. As soon as he went outside, Tommy pushed all of the door locks down. Rather than go directly to the lighthouse, Jonathan went to the back of the car. He opened the trunk, retrieved a tire iron and slammed the trunk shut, absentmindedly forgetting about the noise it would make.

He waved goodbye to Tommy. Jonathan, using whatever terrain he could for concealment, made his way toward the lighthouse. Overhead, the gray overcast sky began to darken. Intermittent sheets of rain pushed against his advance, while the waters of the lake lapped at the rocky shoreline on his right flank. By the time he reached the halfway point he was soaked to his skin. A narrow ribbon of water cut through the land ahead. Fortunately the lake's water level was low, which allowed foot access to the sometimes island.

Although shallow, nevertheless, it was a minor hindrance to his travel. The narrow gap of water required total submersion of his shoes to reach the other side. The cold waters of the lake gnawed at his ankles and the blowing wind chilled him, triggering shivers throughout his body. Having reached the other side, every advancing step produced a squishing sound from his shoes.

***

Ruth and Sheriff Collins finished a late lunch and made their way toward the restaurant's exit. Ruth put on a borrowed slicker she brought along from the sheriff's office. Collins slipped on his poncho and held the door open for her.

"Thanks for lunch, Bob, and the break from the office. I feel a lot better looking for Trevor myself." In contradiction to her announcement, Ruth began to weep. The rain merged with her tears as they walked through the parking lot.

"I sensed you needed to get out," Sheriff Collins said sympathetically before noticing Ruth in the grip of a breakdown. Halting in the rain he grabbed Ruth by her shoulders and looked into her anguished filled eyes. "Frankly, we're both feeling the strain, but you can't give up hope. You have to try to hang on to the thought that we will find Trevor."

Ruth fought to check her sobbing, rubbing the rain and tear mixture from her cheeks. With a quivering chin she nodded back at him, and he released his hold on her shoulders.

Sheriff Collins took Ruth by the arm and guided her to the car. He held the passenger side door open for her and then hurried to the driver's side. Once inside he caught Ruth gazing at him. She reached over and gently touched the top of his hand, which rested on the steering wheel's shift lever.

Self-conscious of the attention, he cleared his throat and awkwardly said, "You better put on your seat belt—this Ford Interceptor's got a lot of muscle under that hood." Blushing slightly, Ruth removed her hand and reached for the nylon seatbelt next to her.

After starting the car, Sheriff Collins grasped the squad's microphone and called his office. "Gary, this is Bob. We're back from lunch. Any new reports?"

The radio squealed and sputtered static. Gary Simons' voice broke through the electrical interference caused by the worsening storm. "Nothing new to report, sheriff, but I got an updated weather report..." More sizzle and snap punctuated his message. "A storm...front is move...in from...northeast, pushing in...heavier rain...of a cold front.

It...pass...by around midnight."

"Gary, I think I got the gist. We're finished in the Sister Bay area. We'll shoot down Fifty-Seven and check out a few of the side roads along the way."

"You're breaking up a bit. Down fif...en...out a few side...the way. Out here."

"Damn! I don't need this," Sheriff Collins barked as he pounded the Motorola mic back onto the car seat. In the distance they could hear the roar of thunder, followed by a crackling sound coming from the radio.

***

Alongside the remnants of *Old Bailey,* a single story, white stucco cottage buttressed its crumbling north end. Wisps of smoke escaped the chimney, only to be pushed downward along the aging sloped roof and toward the open waters of the harbor. Jonathan approached the building on its lee side, sheltered from the blowing northeast storm. A flash of lightning preceded a thunderous boom, which made the saturated ground tremble underfoot.

When he reached the building, Jonathan hugged the outer wall of the structure slowly advancing toward the solitary lit window. Peeking past the weather-coarsened frame, he eyed the interior, progressively widening his view and exposing more of his face to the room's inner glow. Unexpectedly he saw Trevor, apparently doing well, sitting on a wooden chair, across the length of the table from Mister Devlin. They appeared to be engaged in conversation and to Jonathan's disbelief—happy.

Jonathan ducked from view, and considered his next move. He was no stranger to confrontation, having had his share with the aborigines of Africa and South America, but those never involved a crazed clown. Weighing the tire iron in his hand he reassured himself of its advantage in any physical contest.

Leaving his position, he made his way toward the entrance. The eastside of the cottage faced the lake and took the brunt of the storm. A gutter-less roof, functioned as a conduit and channeled sheets of rain over the doorway and formed a shallow moat around the building, creating its own island. Having cursed the rain earlier, he was now thankful for its clatter, which helped cloak his advance. Taking hold of the doorknob he carefully tested its security. He turned the knob and pushed his way in. Rain cascaded down on top of his hat, spilling over its rim onto his shoulders, until he was inside the foyer. He eased his back against the door and gingerly closed it, careful not to let the latch snap and alert his presence.

Another door, windowless and to his right, appeared to be the only one that would open into the modest living room. He steadied himself, reaffirmed his grip on the improvised weapon and bolted into the room, tire iron held high. For a split second he saw Trevor, sitting at the table, startled by his entrance, and then everything went black.

***

Waiting nearly two hours, Tommy began to worry. He thought about sounding the horn, but that would bring attention. He was not certain his uncle would approve. The rain turned into a light mist. Condensation formed on the interior glass and out of boredom, became a canvas for his creative mind. Simple drawings of houses, with disproportionate stick people, coated the transparent gallery. He noted the time on the car's clock at six-thirty and drew a large number seven over his artwork. *This would be the time for action.*

***

The back of Jonathan's head pulsed in pain. Slowly the room began to take shape as he scanned its molten interior. Woozy, he felt the urge to vomit. He tried to move, but the bindings around his arms and legs confirmed that he lost the element of surprise and was now a prisoner. On his left, Trevor sat unemotional and apparently unaware of his uncle's presence. He possessed an unknowing smile. Ahead, a solitary window with a harbor view, presented a bluff-silhouetted horizon, the town within its shadow, bejeweled in electric lights. Behind Jonathan, halfway between the table and his prison chair, the window rattled against the wind.

Struggling to form a sentence, Jonathan labored to ask, "What...do...you want...of...us?"

Mister Devlin did not answer the question. Instead, he mocked Jonathan by grabbing his own head between his white-gloved hands, swaying back and forth, and mimicking pain.

"You...bastard!" Jonathan muttered, while struggling against his bindings, trying unsuccessfully to loosen the straps.

Mister Devlin responded with a broad smile and a swift blow with the back of his hand. A trickle of blood rolled down the side of Jonathan's chin. Unable to physically return the slap, his only option was a slaying glare, to which the demented clown mimed sadness and cleared invisible tears from his murderous eyes.

Mister Devlin went to the credenza, removed a large stained cloth and with great flourish, layered it over the table. He populated its surface with mismatched utensils, plates, and cups. Leaving the room for a few minutes he returned with a large platter and placed it in front of Trevor. Trevor smiled at the sight. Jonathan failed to see anything but an empty serving dish. Obviously beguiled by the demonic buffoon he helped himself to the imaginary banquet. Serving as attendant, the clown selected several logs from a woodpile which was chaotically arranged in the corner, near the fireplace mantle. Throwing them carelessly into the fire, embers swirled about, some escaping up the chimney while others leaped beyond the hearth and onto the stone floor.

As the flames billowed and Trevor indulged in his make-believe repast, Mister Devlin went back to the credenza and retrieved the Wabele mask. Placing it on top his head, the manic jester began to orbit the table, providing some form of entertainment that was perceived by only Trevor. Showing his appreciation, Trevor carefully placed his fork and knife down and then clapped wildly at the bizarre performance. Encouraged by his audience of one, Mister Devlin became more animated in his exaggerated macabre presentation. Contorted shadows quivered over the plaster walls, created from the fire's glow, spawning a menacing Mephistophelean image.

***

"This is not like Jonathan," Ruth said. "He would not leave us worrying. Something is wrong, Bill. We've been here since five-thirty and now it's quarter after six." With each utterance her emotional pitch heightened. All of the daytime patrols were done and nothing new was reported. Besides the sheriff, only two auxiliary deputies were in the office with them. Their eyes followed her as she began to hysterically pace within the office.

Studying the wall map, Sheriff Collins drew an imaginary circle over the northeast section of the county, focusing his attention within its perimeter. He said, "This was his area to canvas. It'll be getting dark soon, so we'll have to hurry if we are to take advantage of any daylight left. Roy, take a squad and swing up to The Point. I'll come up from the south and go north from there."

"I'm on it, Sheriff," said Roy, and left.

Ruth studied him anxiously, pleading with her eyes, she said, "When you say—I'll come up from the south, I hope you mean me, too, Bob?"

"Ruth, if your instincts are correct, I think you should sit this one out."

"But—"

"No! Not this time, Ruth," Sheriff Collins empathetically said, cutting short her fight to accompany him.

Avoiding further eye contact with Ruth, and any opportunity for argument, the sheriff disappeared outside. After opening the patrol car's door he slid onto the driver's side, turned on the ignition and hurriedly backed the car out. Ruth moved to the window and watched as the flashing red dome of the police car faded into the approaching dusk.

***

Tommy closed the car's door and zipped up his jacket. After adjusting the visor on his baseball cap he moved toward the lighthouse point. At first his pace was hesitant, but with each step, he became more focused. He was now on a quest to save his brother and find out why his uncle hadn't returned.

Although the storm had abated and clouds began to thin, the wind off the lake chilled him. When Tommy reached the watery gap in the causeway he hesitated. Without any stepping-stones, he would have to get his leather shoes wet; something his mother always warned him against doing. Briefly considering his dilemma, he quickly removed them and his socks, rolled his cuffed jeans up to his knees. He carefully walked across the rock-strewn trench. When he reached the other side he reversed the process, donning shoes over his now dampened socks.

Looking forward, the skeletal frame of the lighthouse was barely visible through the scattering of trees ahead. Zigzagging his way through the labyrinth, Tommy panted, both from activity and nervous anticipation of what he would do if confronted by Mister Devlin.

Tired, and now within fifty feet of the house, Tommy paused. He caught his breath and contemplated his next move. The cloud-muted sun hovered low behind the elevated ridge of the community on the far side of the bay. As twilight descended over the harbor, the shadowy blue silhouette of the town began to fade, replaced by the lights from homes and streetlamps. Moving toward the window, Tommy's face became partially illuminated by the glowing interior. He gasped in disbelief at what he saw and quickly retreated back into the shadow beyond the window frame.

Tommy's body quaked with shock seeing his brother and uncle under the obvious control of the fiendish clown. He knew, when he first saw him at the circus, he was evil. Now, paralyzed with fear, his mind reeled in terror. He realized how dangerous this foe was.

Out of the corner of his eye, he caught some movement. His heart raced with fright at the thought that Mister Devlin, sensing his presence, had now come to take him, too. An unnerving form came out of the advancing shadows of the sunset and approached Tommy. Unrecognizable at first, until it was within reach of the window's glow. He identified the phantom intruder as the stranger he saw on the beach, almost two weeks ago.

Unlike the day Tommy saw the stranger near the lighthouse, where the apparition made no acknowledgement, this time he looked directly into Tommy's eyes. Frozen in dread of him, Tommy recoiled at his gaping head injury and nearly cried out in fear. The man, wearing the same wet work clothes he wore on the beach, calmly pacified Tommy with soothing waves of his arms. He gestured to Tommy, pointing to small rocks heaped alongside the building.

Puzzled by the significance of the stones, Tommy raised his arms and shoulders in question. Pretending to pick up one, the man hurled the imaginary projectile into the night air. He repeated the motion several more times. Finally, grasping the point of the charade, Tommy smiled in acknowledgement while the apparition grinned in return.

With renewed confidence, Tommy hastily gathered stones, filling every pocket of his jacket and jeans with the new found ammunition. Going back to the cottage entrance he slipped inside, careful not to make a sound. Seeing the second door on his right, he peeked through the keyhole to check out the situation inside.

His view was limited, seeing only Trevor, sitting with his back to the fireplace. Occasionally, Mister Devlin would flit past the keyhole's reach. Listening and studying his rotations inside, rocks in hand, Tommy waited for the right moment to burst into the room.

***

"Roy?" The sheriff's voice broke through the radio's background static. "Where are you?"

"Sheriff, I'm about four miles north of town, on fifty-seven."

"Meet me at the junction of Q and fifty-seven. We'll both check out Ridges Road and the Point Road." His voice was gravelly from dehydration and fatigue. Sounds from his stomach also reminded him that he hadn't eaten since lunch.

"Roger. Out," replied Roy.

Sheriff Collins turned down the squelch on his radio and pondered the approaching evening. Overhead, clouds began to part, revealing a few of the higher magnitude stars. Halfway over the horizon, the moon, three-quarter full, was centered like a large pearl between the diamond-like planets of Jupiter and Saturn. He appreciated the beauty, but struggled against accepting it amid the death and sadness of the past couple of weeks.

Parked on the shoulder of the intersecting gravel roads, the sheriff flashed his headlights twice, signaling his approaching deputy to stop. Replying in kind, Roy turned onto the secondary road and parked opposite the sheriff's car.

Deputy Adams walked across the road and met the sheriff, who was laying out a map of Door County on the damp hood of his squad car.

Using his flashlight he pointed to the east side of the harbor. "I want you to check out all side roads and driveways on the north side of Ridges Road while I do the south side. Once we get here," he pointed to the intersection of Point Drive and Ridges Road, "we'll meet up again, and travel together the rest of the way to the point."

"Okay, Sheriff. Do you want rolling reports?"

"No, only if you see something suspicious. Now, let's get going," Collins said and moved hastily toward the driver's side of his squad car.

With headlights leading the way, each vehicle's spotlight obliquely scrutinized the passing landscape along the roadway. Methodically moving forward, their lights whipped at the darkened recesses of the forest and cottages. The beams stirred feral cats, triggered dogs into barking, and deer froze in its glare. Occasionally, the curious would venture outside and stare at the passing procession in bewilderment.

***

Slowly turning the doorknob, Tommy pushed inward, clearing the latch bolt beyond the mortise of the strike plate. Holding two larger rocks in his left hand, he grabbed one of them with his right hand. He forcibly pushed the unrestricted door in with his shoulder.

For a split second, time stopped. Mister Devlin spun around so quickly that the Wabele mask fell to the ground. Tommy, standing, framed in the open doorway, drew back and hurled one of his rocks at the startled clown, striking him in the temple. Dazed from the blow, Mister Devlin teetered backward. Tommy flipped the second stone from his left hand into his right and launched another missile, this time hitting the crazy joker between the eyes. Jacket pockets bulging with ammunition, Tommy continued to pelt Mister Devlin as he tried to regain his footing.

Slithering behind the seated Trevor, who was still oblivious to the danger, Mister Devlin pulled on the chair. Dragging his way up, he cowered behind Trevor, using him as a human shield from Tommy's hail of rocks.

Moving toward Jonathan, Tommy broke off his salvo of stones and retrieved his Cub Scout knife from his rear pocket. After cutting his uncle's wrist restraints, he gave the knife back to him. Jonathan leaned forward in his chair, cutting through the remaining tether around his ankles. He became dizzy and fell forward onto the floor.

Weak, yet determined, Jonathan urged Tommy, "Take the tablecloth—cover yourself with it—and wear the Wabele mask. Don't worry about me—just do it! Send him back—Tommy. Send him back."

Fearing his predicament, Mister Devlin grabbed Trevor and pulled him to his feet. Keeping Trevor between Tommy and himself, he inched his way backwards towards the fireplace.

Tommy instinctively knew he only had one chance at this standoff. He pulled the tablecloth free of the table, scattering plates, cups and platters onto the stone floor. He took back his knife from Jonathan. Having learned from his first experience in the attic, he quickly cut a hole in the center of the sheet and slid the knife back towards his uncle. Although crude, it was sufficient for him to see through.

It was a contest of time. Mister Devlin abruptly turned Trevor toward the roaring fire and mimicked throwing him into the blaze. Tormenting his adversaries with his sinister threat, looking over his shoulder and back into the room, he smiled mockingly. He goaded them into testing his resolve.

Jonathan, having regained his equilibrium, slashed and sawed at his bindings, frantically working to free himself. Cutting through one section of rope the remaining turns around his ankles fell to the ground. Kicking them away, he slowly regained his strength and began to crawl toward Mister Devlin. From his prone position he mustered all the energy he could and yelled, "The mask Tommy, put on the mask!"

Tommy, wrapped in the dirty tablecloth, pulled at it until he was able to align the jagged opening with his eyes. He saw the Wabele mask lying on the floor on the opposite side of the table. Dropping to the ground, he scrambled under the table to retrieve it. As he crawled headfirst to the other side his knees became entangled in the sheet and Tommy fell blindly onto the stone floor. He panicked. His arms and legs moving wildly under the sheet as he frantically sought any opening that he could use to see through. He found the flap of the hem and regained his bearings. He scampered to the other side of the table. Not bothering to stand, Tommy readjusted the cloth so he could peek through the ragged hole. He hurriedly donned the mask, shouting, "Trevor! Trevor! Get away from him!"

Trevor came out from the veil of confusion imposed on him through Mister Devlin's sorcery. He suddenly became conscious of his surroundings. Terrified, feeling the heat from the flames, he tried to break loose from the clown's grip. He strained to wrench his arm free. The clown would not yield his hold.

Jonathan sprang from his half-kneeling position. He collided with the vindictive fool, shoving him towards the gaping hearth. Mister Devlin began to lose his balance. Teetering near the fireplace's opening, Jonathan struggled with the clown trying to free Trevor from Devlin's grasp.

Jonathan pulled Trevor toward himself, while at the same time shoving Mister Devlin backwards into the fireplace. The flames embraced the clown. Like fiery tentacles they dragged him further into the flaming chasm.

Seeing the clown's fate, Tommy cried out, "Go back to where you came from!" Making certain of his intention to rid the world of Mister Devlin, he repeated the exorcism. "Go back—go back to where you came from!" he shouted.

Orange flames flayed at Mister Devlin. His screams, if any, where overcome by a demonic howl that swirled within the inferno as they whipped around his thrashing body. His clown costume ignited. The grisly silhouette revealed a hideous outline of sinew metamorphosing into an emaciated bonelike frame. The remnants tottered, collapsed and billowed, flaring into a giant fireball.

Jonathan went to Tommy, who was hypnotized at the sight. He removed the Wabele mask from him and threw it, too, into the fireplace, ending the death mask's juju.

Trevor, now fully aware of what was happening, helped remove the tablecloth from his brother. He looked at his uncle and asked, "What about this?"

He snatched the fabric from Trevor, balled it up, and tossed it into the flames. It suddenly combusted, pushing flaming pieces of material into the room. Rising embers fled to the rafters and seized the desiccated beams, igniting them so swiftly that it took everyone by surprise.

"Quick, let's get outta here!" Jonathan urged. Grabbing his beat up hat from the floor, he herded them outdoors. Slowly the smoke seeped through the weathered soffits, licking at the fascia. Soon they gave way to fingers of flames that progressed upward toward the roof's peak. The center of the roof exploded into a flash of fire.

Seeking a safe distance, the three of them moved rapidly north along the narrow peninsula to their car and safety. They paused at the slender channel of water that intersected their path. Tommy and Trevor dropped to the ground and began to untie their leather shoes.

"What are you two doing?" Jonathan asked incredulously.

"Mom said we shouldn't get our shoes wet. So we are taking them off," Tommy responded.

"Forget that. Tie them back up. I'm sure your mother won't mind this time. If she says anything, blame me," Jonathan cajoled.

***

"Sheriff!" Roy yelled into his car radio's microphone.

"What's up, Roy?"

"It looks like we got us a fire ahead. And it appears to be at the *Old Bailey Light*."

Shifting his attention to the point, Sheriff Collins confirmed Roy's deduction. "Yep, I see it. I'll call it in. Let's see what that's all about." After changing frequencies, he flipped on his red-dome light, pushed on the car's accelerator, and raced toward the source. With one hand on the steering wheel and the other on his microphone, he called in the fire alarm.

Sheriff Collins pulled alongside of his deputy's car; both vehicles' lights illuminated Ruth's Nash Ambassador. He turned on his spotlight and scanned the area. Seeing nothing of Jonathan or Tommy, he opened the car's door. With flashlight in one hand and his revolver in the other he investigated on foot. Leaving the red dome light on, he joined Deputy Adams, who began walking south over the rocky terrain and sparsely wooded isthmus.

Unsure of the danger in calling out, they remained cautiously silent. Flaying at the night with their flashlights they moved in the direction of the burning lighthouse. Backlit by the fire, Sheriff Collins spotted three moving silhouettes walking toward him. By their size, he surmised them to be Jonathan, Tommy, and Trevor. He enthusiastically called out. "Jonathan?"

"Hello! It's Jonathan. I've got the boys with me," his voice heavy with fatigue. "We're okay."

Lit by flashlight beams, they emerged from the tree line bedraggled as they closed the gap between them. Tommy and Trevor, squinting into the lights, broke ranks and rushed toward the rays.

"Is anyone hurt?" Sheriff Collins asked.

"Uncle Jonathan is. That clown hit him on the head—tied him up—" Tommy, overexcited, began to chatter on.

"Whoa, take it easy, Tommy!" Sheriff Collins advised. "We'll get to all that later." His words were calming as he advanced on Jonathan to check on his condition. "How you doing?"

"I think I'm okay, but I got knocked out—had a dizzy spell and felt like throwing up." Jonathan waved off the concerns, trying to minimize the attention the sheriff was giving him.

"Sounds like you have a concussion." Taking his flashlight, the sheriff examined Jonathan's eyes. "Sure enough, your eyes are dilated. We'll get you an ambulance," he said, sounding alarmed. While leading him to his squad car the sheriff inquired about Mister Devlin.

"You don't have to worry about him anymore. He's dead," Jonathan said, with finality. In the distance, the sound of approaching sirens increased in intensity.

***

Ruth stood bedside, while the doctor examined her brother. Tommy and Trevor remained in the waiting room, impatiently skimming through dog-eared magazines, eager to leave the hospital.

"I would say you were very lucky," remarked the doctor, as he removed the stethoscope from Jonathan's chest. "Your vitals appear normal, but I would advise you not to drive for a couple of days—to be on the safe side."

"Don't worry, doc. He'll be under my care," Ruth assured, her face free of the anxiety she wore over the last several days.

"I'll send in the nurse. She'll have some forms for you to sign. After that, you are free to go. Just take it easy," the doctor cautioned and left the room.

"It's been quite a vacation," Jonathan quipped.

Returning his smile, Ruth said, "Not one you'll want to do again."

"You got that right, Sis."

"Bob! what a pleasant surprise," Ruth chirped, as Sheriff Collins entered the room.

"I came here to check on Jonathan, and to see if there is anything I can do. How are you doing, Deputy Morrison?" Sheriff Collins asked, looking concerned.

"Pretty good, sheriff, but it's back to being an archaeologist. I've gotten a clean bill of health and I'm checking out today," he said with a sigh of relief. "Still got the bump on my noggin; Mister Devlin did pack one heck of a wallop."

"Speaking of Mister Devlin, the forensic people from Madison searched the site and didn't find any evidence of a body—not even a bone. The chief investigator informed me that a body would burn at around 600 degrees Fahrenheit, but it would take 1400 to 1800 degrees to vaporize all organic matter—even bones." Scrunching up his face, he added, "That's damn hot."

"I don't know about the level of heat, but it was extremely hot when he fell into the hearth and burst into flame," Jonathan explained.

"Well, anyway, the lab boys collected samples of the ash and will be doing some further tests," Sheriff Collins soothed, not appearing to question Jonathan's judgment. "Ruth, how about if I give the boys a ride home in my squad car? I'm sure they would enjoy it. It'll give you and your brother a little private time."

"That would be great, Bob. The boys have been through quite an ordeal and your counselling would be welcome, too. I'm concerned about what influence everything had on them. In fact, why don't you have dinner with us tonight? It will give all of us a chance at some normalcy," Ruth's tone overflowed with anticipative optimism. "We'll have a cookout," she added.

"You don't have to ask me twice," he said, exchanging smiles with her. "Well, I'm going to be on my way. See you later." After receiving a parting hug from Ruth and a handshake from Jonathan, Sheriff Collins disappeared into the hallway.

"Sis, I would venture to say that man is sweet on you," her brother teased.

"Yes, I know," she said cheerfully.

***

Heading north, the sheriff and the twins relived the events of the past couple of weeks. They recalled the heroism of their uncle and dramatic escape. Prodded by the twins, he turned on the car's siren a couple of times when they were alone on the highway, entertaining their curiosity. He realized that in spite of the triumph, many wounds would take time to heal, including his own. He was determined to do all he could to help Ruth and her boys.

Tommy sat in the rear seat on the passenger side of the car and looked lazily to his right. The dense forest thinned as they approached Jacksonport. In the distance, beyond a whitewashed spired church, a graveyard, populated with markers, mysteriously glimmered under the noonday sun.

ABOUT THE AUTHOR

Christopher Malinger lives with his wife Eileen, in Central Florida. His most recent work, *The Object of Desire*, appeared in *Journeys VII*; an Anthology of Award-Winning Short Stories, Published in 2014. Also, a winner in the Florida Writers Association Adult Collection, Volume 7, *The Sweet Scent of Spring; published in 2015*. Other works include a collection of short stories, *Tales to Keep You Awake, The Back Roads of Terror,* and his novella, *The Wabele*. He is a member of the Florida Writers Association.

www.christophermalinger.com

www.ingramcontent.com/pod-product-compliance
Lightning Source LLC
Chambersburg PA
CBHW070503130626
46555CB00003B/1137